Title: Boy in a White R

Author: Karl Olsber

Translated by: Larisa Villar Hauser

On-Sale Date: February 7, 2023

Format: Jacketed Hardcover

ISBN: 978-1-338-83184-9 ‖ Price: $18.99 US

Ages: 12 and up

Grades: 7 and up

LOC Number: Available

Length: 256 pages

Trim: 5-1/2 x 8-1/4 inches

Classification:

Thriller & Suspense (F)

Technology (F)

Science Fiction (F)

----------------- *Additional Formats Available* --------------

Ebook ISBN: 978-1-338-83185-6

ChickenHouse

An Imprint of Scholastic Inc.
557 Broadway, New York, NY 10012
For information, contact us at:
tradepublicity@scholastic.com

BOY IN A
WHITE ROOM

BOY IN A WHITE ROOM

KARL OLSBERG

Translated by Larisa Villar Hauser

Chicken House

Scholastic Inc. / *New York*

Library of Congress Cataloging-in-Publication Data available

ISBN 978-1-338-83184-9

10 9 8 7 6 5 4 3 2 1   23 24 25 26 27

Printed in U.S.A   66

First edition, February 2023

Book design by Abby Dening

For Nik

I will suppose then not that God, who is sovereignly good and the fountain of truth, but that some malignant demon, who is at once exceedingly powerful and deceitful, has employed all his artifice to deceive me; I will suppose that the sky, the air, the earth, colors, figures, sounds, and all external things, are nothing better than the illusions of dreams by means of which this being has devised to ensnare my judgment. I will consider myself as without hands, eyes, flesh, blood or any of the senses, and as falsely believing that I am possessed of these; I will continue resolutely fixed in this belief, and if indeed by these means it be not in my power to arrive at the knowledge of truth, I shall at least do what is in my power, that is, suspend my judgment and guard with settled purpose against giving my assent to what is false, and being imposed upon by this deceiver, whatever be his power and artifice!

RENÉ DESCARTES,
Meditations on First Philosophy,
1641

CHAPTER 1

Where am I?

A white cube-shaped room. No lights, but the walls seem to glow and I can make out the faint outline of their edges. No windows or doors, no furniture, no pictures on the walls. Nothing to tell me what there is outside these walls or how I got here. Total silence.

Who am I?

No name springs to mind, no sense of self, only concepts: I know what dice are, a tree, a dog, a computer. But none of that stuff connects to me. I can't relate it to any of my own experiences. I don't even know where the concepts come from. I remember *nothing*.

I stare at my hands in awe. They look like they're covered in thin plastic gloves that hide the fine lines and ridges of my fingertips. I'm wearing a glossy white jumpsuit and stroke the fabric, but feel nothing—my fingertips feel nothing and I can't feel the pressure of my hand against my leg. I hit myself hard but don't feel any pain. I've lost my sense of touch. And I can't smell anything either.

I slowly go to a wall and reach out my hand, touch the flat surface, but again feel nothing. The wall is solid. I search along it for a hidden switch, a crack, anything that might reveal an opening, but there's no way out. I start to panic. What's happening? Who's locked me in and why? Did I do something wrong? I can't remember. My heart must be racing but I don't feel it. What's wrong with me?

I try kicking the wall but can't feel or hear the impact. It's like I don't exist.

Maybe I'm dreaming? But if this is a dream, then it's scarily real. The silence is oppressive, as though nothing exists outside this room. A terrifying thought.

"Hey! Let me out!" I yell. At least, I try to yell, but all that comes out of my mouth is a strange monotone that sounds like it's computer-generated.

"I don't understand the command." A woman's voice. She sounds just as fake as I do. Her voice seems to come from everywhere. Even so, I look back, half hopeful, half scared, that someone has magically appeared, that there's a way in and therefore a way out. But there's no one.

"What?" I ask.

"I don't understand the question," she says.

"Who . . . who are you?"

"My name is Alice," the voice replies. "It stands for Advanced Language Interpretation Counseling Extension."

"Where am I?"

"I am not authorized to disclose information about your location or your status."

"Who am I?"

"You are the patient."

The word triggers bleak images. "Am I in the hospital?"

"I am not authorized to disclose information about your location or your status."

"So what are you authorized to do? What's happening? Why am I here?"

"I am here to help you find out about your new environment."

I don't understand what's going on. Is this some kind of sick joke? A scientific experiment? Or some new kind of therapy? Maybe I'm not in a regular hospital but in a mental clinic. Maybe they've given me drugs to wipe out my memory, numb my senses, and make my voice sound flat. Whatever's going on, I want out. I have to get out!

"Please, let me out of here!"

"I don't understand the command. Say 'help' to hear information about my basic functions."

"Help."

"Welcome. My name is Alice, which is an acronym for 'Advanced Language Interpretation Counseling Extension.' I am here to help you find your way around your new environment. I respond to simple commands or answer questions. I recognize the commands 'show me,' 'what is,' 'where is,' 'open,' and 'close.'"

"Open the door."

"I don't understand the command."

"What is outside this room?"

"I don't understand the question."

"Damn it! Just tell me what happened to me!"

"I don't understand the command. Say 'help' to hear information about my basic functions."

Frustrated, I hit the wall with my fist. The fact that I don't feel anything just makes things worse.

"Help!" I shout, confused. My voice is lifeless, and the computer gives its standard response.

I pace up and down my prison restlessly, like a tiger in a cage. Over time, the space seems to shrink, as though the glowing walls are closing in on me. I measure the room in equal-sized steps, over and over—it's only five paces from one side to the other. Even though the distance doesn't change, I still feel like there's less and less space. The air seems to get thinner.

I can't afford to freak out! I have to pull myself together, focus and be methodical if I want to find out what's going on. *Deep breath.* I try to concentrate on my breathing, but can't feel my lungs. I can't breathe! My head spins and for a second I feel like I'm going to pass out, but nothing happens.

Stay calm! Wherever I am, there's no immediate danger. There has to be an explanation for all this. I feel encouraged by that thought.

"How did I get here?" I ask the computer voice.

"I don't understand the question."

"What is this room?"

"This room is a computer simulation, what is known as virtual reality."

Of course. Why didn't I think of that? I know all about virtual worlds. A list of games springs to mind: *Minecraft, World of Warcraft, League of Legends, Team Defense, Assassin's Creed.* I've probably played them often, even though I don't remember much about them.

Maybe someone has put a VR headset on me and fed me drugs so that I forget who and where I am. But who would do that? And why?

I touch my face but can't feel anything. I turn my head and see a different section of the room. I walk up and down, even jump on the spot, without creating any disturbances or time lags. And I don't see any pixels. If I am wearing a VR headset it must be really high spec.

"Is this a computer game?"

"A computer game is a software program that enables one or more users to play a game interactively according to set rules. Would you like more information?"

I wonder whose idea it was to call this dumb program "advanced." "Am I in a computer game?"

"I am not authorized to disclose information about your location or your status."

If this is a game, then my task must be to find a way out of this room. But how? There don't seem to be any kind of unlocking mechanisms, so my only option is to talk to Alice. Maybe I need to find a code word that opens the door or something.

I try a direct approach. "Tell me the code word."

"I don't understand the command."

Asking questions doesn't seem to get me anywhere. What were the commands Alice understood? "Show me," "open," "close."

I take a punt and say: "Show me elephants!" Surprisingly, Alice actually understands. Three columns and four lines of elephant videos appear on the walls. Most of them seem to come from webcams inside elephant enclosures at zoos. It's easy to spot the pixelated structure and streaks that are typical of a video stream downloading via a low-bandwidth internet connection. I tap one of the pictures with my index finger and it expands to fill most of the wall while the other pictures shrink and move down to the bottom.

There's a location name at the top of the picture—the elephant enclosure is in a Dutch zoo—and there's a time stamp too: 10:15, April 27, 2017. Some of the other cameras show location and time details too, so I can tell the videos are being streamed. I still don't know where I am but at least I know the date. As though that's any help.

Still, I seem to have an internet connection. This sheds a whole new light on the other commands Alice understands.

"Open Google!"

The elephant pictures disappear and the walls turn white. The wall in front of me now shows a web browser with the search engine's home page. I tap the search field and a cursor blinks. The walls are giant touch screens but there's no virtual keyboard.

"Elephant," I say loudly. The word immediately shows up in the Google search field. I tap the search button and, as expected, a list of search results, pictures, and information appears.

I'm in a simulated room with virtual touch screens that give me access to the internet. What's the point of all this? And how come I know how Google works but don't remember ever having used the search engine?

"Open Google Earth."

The wall shows a satellite picture. The dark strip of a river trails across the gray-green surface from top left to bottom right. In the center of the screen, the river forks, then joins up again, forming an onion-shaped island. The image around the river is made of gray pixels, as though someone has sprayed ash everywhere. I know this place, even without the white writing in the middle of the picture—but I don't know why. Google determines a location using an IP address, then shows the corresponding satellite image. I know this too, though I don't know how. But it really helps narrow down my location.

"Am I in Hamburg?" I ask.

"I am not authorized to disclose information about your location or your status," Alice replies without emotion.

"Show me Hamburg," I instruct Alice.

The map and search screen disappear and are replaced by

dozens of webcams. They show different areas of the city: the Inner Alster with its fountains, the jetties, the Port of Hamburg, the Elbe Philharmonic, the station, the airport, lots of streets that I don't immediately recognize. Cars whiz across the screen, people walk around purposefully. I so badly want to be in their shoes, being filmed by cameras instead of here in this virtual room watching an image of a world that's out of reach.

Who am I? Where am I? Why am I here? My questions become more urgent by the second.

Maybe one of the camera pictures will trigger a memory. Even though I recognize a lot of the distinctive buildings and places, it feels like I've only ever watched a film about Hamburg without actually having been there myself. My attention is drawn to one of the video streams. There's nothing special to see—a tarmac cycle path in a residential street next to a park—but the camera angle is unusual: the image moves down the street, more or less at eye level, turning sometimes left, sometimes right, as though filmed by a drunk cameraman whizzing past trees, pedestrians, and parked cars. In the top right-hand corner of the video there's a logo for an internet company: Eyestream.

The image suddenly veers downward and I see the tip of a skateboard racing along the cycle path. The camera must be attached to a skateboarder's head.

"Alice, open Eyestream!"

The webcam pictures disappear and a sleek website opens. It shows a number of videos with a similar sort of perspective, except they're moving a lot more slowly—they must come from cameras being carried by people walking. The streamers' names and locations are shown: Carol in Amsterdam, George in Trondheim, Ralf in Pisa, Maria in Regensburg.

A short description explains how Eyestream "lets the world share your life by livestreaming everything you see." But only if you want to, of course—and strictly in compliance with data protection regulation. The service already has over three hundred thousand members, but only a little over one thousand cameras are currently active. I was just watching one.

I enter "Hamburg" into the search field and get four more matches. When I click the top one, the site asks me to register. Great. Username? I have no idea what my name is. I enter "Boy in a White Room." My email address? I can't remember. So I open Google and get myself a new one: boyinawhiteroom@gmail.com.

Once I've completed registration, I pick a stream and it fills the screen. It belongs to Mike, a twenty-one-year-old student who is strolling down Mönckeberg Street toward city hall. I can hear muffled street sounds through his microphone: voices, a busker.

Just as I'm about to click to another stream, I hear loud, harsh voices. Mike turns his head and I see an elderly man wearing shabby clothes sitting in a doorway with his decrepit-looking dog. Two young men wearing leather jackets stand in front of him. I can't make out what they're saying but it's obvious they're swearing and giving the man a hard time.

He covers his head with his hands. Only now do I realize the camera isn't moving. Mike has stopped to watch.

People appear at the edge of the picture. A crowd of spectators has gathered but nobody steps in to help the man.

"Do something!" I shout.

"I don't understand the command," says Alice.

"Alice, call the police!"

"I don't understand the command."

At that moment one of the thugs throws a beer bottle at the homeless man. It smashes: there's glass everywhere, a cut trailing blood down the homeless man's face. The scraggy dog barks loudly but the man holds it back as the attackers howl with laughter. The dog jumps up and snaps at the assailant's arm. He stumbles back, screaming in pain. The animal is biting down on his leather jacket and won't let go. In a swift move, the second man kills the dog with a switchblade.

Nobody helps. People just stand and stare. I have to do something. Anything!

I can send messages to Eyestream users by accessing a chat function. But it's already too late: the old man is sobbing over his dead dog while the assailants run off and the crowd of gawkers disperses. Mike moves away too and just keeps on walking. I hear his voice:

"Man, that was gross. Did you see? A couple of guys just beat up a homeless man and stabbed his dog. I reckon I'll be right up there for Stream of the Month. So, thumbs-up—vote for me, okay?"

I feel like puking and type into the chat window: *Phone the police, you asshole!*

Mike doesn't react. Disgusted, I ask Alice to close Eyestream.

For a while, I just stare at the white walls. I feel sick. I'm not sure whether it's from staring at the moving pictures, the gory scene I've just witnessed, or my sense of utter helplessness. I shake off my stupor and pace around the white room again—agitated, helpless, frustrated—until my thoughts settle.

What do I know so far? I'm in a virtual room with no way out. I've lost my memory and don't know where my body is. I can see into the outside world through a thousand pairs of eyes, but it's pointless unless I know where to look. Then there's Alice, the artificial wannabe-intelligence. She is most likely my best lead.

"Open Google!"

I click the search box and enter "Alice." The search results show references to Lewis Carroll's book *Alice's Adventures in Wonderland*. I know the book even though I don't remember ever having read it. Other than that, a singer and a suffragette appear on the first page. There's no mention of a software program by that name. But that would have been way too easy.

Next, I enter "Advanced Language Interpretation Counseling Extension."

Google finds various matches for "Advanced Counseling" or "Language Interpretation," but nothing for a software program that understands simple voice commands. So that's no use either.

I try "Artificial Intelligence Hamburg."

The top match is the website for a company called Mycrologic, which deals with the development of algorithms for something called data mining, whatever that is. There's nothing on the home page to suggest the company designed Alice. But that doesn't necessarily mean a thing.

"Who is Mycrologic?" I ask Alice.

"Mycrologic is a leading service provider in the analysis and processing of big data by means of neural networks," she answers helpfully. "Mycrologic's clients include internationally renowned companies such as Philips, Siemens, Deutsche Telekom, Commerzbank, DKV, BMW, and Vattenfall. Mycrologic— we'll find any needle in your data haystack."

Interesting: Alice, who doesn't seem to know much about anything, knows a whole lot about Mycrologic. Maybe it's worth taking a closer look at the company website.

At first glance I don't see anything interesting—no systems like Alice, no computer simulations or virtual worlds. The company seems to develop software that makes it possible to search large amounts of data for patterns and links in order to better predict user behavior. So that's what data mining is. When I enter "Mycrologic" into Google, an article appears that was published in a business magazine in 2013. It reports how millionaire Henning Jaspers bought a "double-digit" million euro stake in the company.

Something about the name feels familiar, as though I've heard it before, but it doesn't come with any specific knowledge, and definitely no memories. On the other hand, Google and Wikipedia know a lot about Henning Jaspers. He founded the company Dark Star with his partner Marten Raffay, and they achieved worldwide success with the mega-hit game *Team Defense*. Maybe that's why I know his name.

I stumble across an eight-month-old newspaper report:

WIFE OF HAMBURG MILLIONAIRE SHOT BY INTRUDERS

Hamburg. On Saturday night, unidentified intruders broke into the mansion of internet entrepreneur Henning Jaspers. The millionaire's wife, Maria Jaspers, was shot during the break-in. His fifteen-year-old son was injured and is in critical condition. He has been transferred to a specialist clinic. According to investigating officers, evidence suggests that the perpetrators intended to abduct the young man but were interrupted by his mother, who used pepper spray to fight them off. At least two people were involved. Speaking on behalf of the family, Henning Jaspers's lawyer stated that the entrepreneur will not be available for comment at this time. He will, however, do everything he can to support the police in their efforts to solve this appalling crime. If you have any information, please report it to your local police station.

The article shows a photograph of a luxury villa. It's impossible to make out the faces of the people in the picture. I click to enlarge it. Have I been there before? I don't remember.

"Who is Henning Jaspers?" I ask.

"Henning Jaspers is your father," says Alice.

CHAPTER 2

The browser closes even though I haven't asked it to. The walls turn white and a spinning hourglass appears. When it vanishes, I suddenly find myself in some kind of library. It isn't just projected onto the virtual walls of the white room but is a totally realistic three-dimensional setting, as though I've been teleported here.

What just happened? I look around. Tall bookshelves rise up on all sides; windows look out onto a large garden. A big, modern desk made of dark wood dominates the room. Two leather chairs stand in a corner. A door leads out.

I try taking a step forward. I can move around this room normally. But my hands, like the rest of me, are still a virtual projection. I try taking a book from the shelf, but can't.

I'm not actually here, wherever *here* is.

The door opens with a quiet squeak and a man walks in. He's around fifty years old, with gray-flecked, thinning hair and a big nose with a pair of glasses perched on it. Although his features are highly detailed, I can immediately tell he's just a virtual reality configuration, like me.

"Manuel!" His voice sounds happy, but his virtual face wears only a thin, stiff smile. He comes toward me to give me a hug. Then stops when he realizes how pointless that would be in a virtual world. "How are you, Manuel?"

Manuel. The name sounds familiar somehow, but not *so* familiar that it feels like my name.

"Who are you?" I say.

His face is expressionless. "You still don't remember anything?" Unlike my voice and Alice's, his sounds natural, and I can hear his disappointment. He's a real person.

"No," I answer.

"That's what I was worried about," he says resignedly. "I'm sorry, son. We did everything to stabilize your memory, but your brain keeps rejecting the implants."

That doesn't sound good. "What implants?"

"One thing at a time. You're here, which means you've found out who you are."

"Alice said I'm the son of the millionaire Henning Jaspers. I guess that's you."

He looks at me for a second without speaking. I realize that I may have hurt his feelings. When he finally speaks, his voice shows no emotion: "Yes, that's me. You're my son, Manuel, even if you don't remember me. I must seem like a stranger to you and yet you're the only thing I still care about." He pauses for a second, as though trying to find the right words. "Those pigs killed your mother and wrecked your life. They'll pay for that!"

"So is it true, what it says online? Intruders . . . shot my mother?"

"Of course it's true. Why do you think I need to talk to you from inside this virtual world, instead of holding you in my arms in the real world?"

"That's what I don't understand. Where am I? What's wrong with me?"

"I'll show you," he says, and moves his hand.

A second later I'm no longer inside the library but in a white-painted room with a linoleum floor and a hospital bed next to shelves full of flashing electronic machines. A thick cable runs toward the head of a young man lying on the bed: he's around fifteen years old, with curly dark hair sticking out of a net cap made of thin wires. Tubes run into his mouth and nose. His eyes are closed, his face relaxed, as though he's sleeping peacefully.

For a short while, I stare dumbly at the lifeless form, then move closer and lean down over him. "That . . . that's me?"

The avatar of the man who claims to be my father nods. "The bullet hit you in the neck. Your spine was shattered. Splinters of bone lodged in your brain stem. It's a miracle you survived."

Seriously? Is that really me? It doesn't feel that way. But then I've probably never seen my body from the outside.

"Those wires go straight into my brain?" What a freakish idea.

"Yes. Your mind is totally separate from your body. Not even the nerve signals from your eyes and ears reach your brain. The only thing that works is your blood circulation. The doctors said you were as good as dead, but when we examined your brain we could still see activity. It took us a while, but we managed to decode the key nerve signals so that you are able to control your virtual body. The hardest bit was trying to decode your language center. But as you see, we did that too. Your voice is computer-generated but the words are yours. You were trapped inside a dark prison and we got you out."

I look around the virtual hospital room. This isn't what freedom looks like to me.

"Will I ever be able to use my body again?"

He hesitates. I can tell from his voice that he's close to tears when he says: "No. No, son, that's not going to happen. I wish I could tell you something different."

"I understand." But do I really? I feel as though I've been kicked in the head. To live in this virtual reality world forever . . . maybe losing my memory isn't my brain rejecting electrodes, but its way of rejecting the bleak truth.

"Come, I have something to show you." He moves a hand and the hospital room disappears. Now I find myself in a room with sloping walls and a pitched roof—a converted attic, I think. A computer stands on a desk; there's a shelf full of books next to it, a wardrobe, a bed. A poster of a band whose name I recognize even though none of their music comes to mind. Over the bed hangs a scene from the film *The Lord of the Rings*: Frodo leans on the railings of Elrond's palace and stares out over magical Rivendell. Above that, there's a signed picture of the HSV team, Hamburg's biggest football club—apparently I was a fan. A tennis racket lies next to a rucksack that spills schoolbooks onto the floor. Everything seems so real, and yet so alien.

"This is your room," he explains. "We made it exactly the way it was when . . ." He falters. After a while he asks: "Do you remember anything at all?"

In no way do I feel as though I've been in this room before. None of the stuff means anything to me. I can name the football players in the poster, but can't say whether or not I've ever kicked a football. I know who Elrond and Frodo are and know what happens in the film but don't know when or where I watched it. I suddenly feel like I'm looking at something incredibly precious—a prized possession that's out of reach: the life I used to have.

"I don't know," I say, hiding my confusion.

"It may still come back." But his voice doesn't sound hopeful. "So, I've got another surprise for you. I mean, there have to be some advantages to living in a virtual world."

He touches the *Lord of the Rings* poster and then I'm standing next to a curved balustrade expertly crafted out of light-colored wood, looking out over a wooded valley with steep rock faces and tumbling waterfalls. A sweeping bridge spans a waterfall in a graceful arc and sunlight forms a rainbow in the spray.

"Wow!" I can't help saying.

"Do you like it?" As I turn toward him, I can see he looks

different. He's wearing a long tunic, his hair falls over his shoulders, and his face is distinctly younger. Even his glasses are gone. But the most striking difference has to be the pointed ears.

"We got the original files from Peter Jackson, the ones that were used for the film's 3D animations and sets," he says proudly. "Of course, we had to majorly enhance them to make the areas accessible."

"Did you . . . you did all this for me?"

His elf face shows no emotion. "I wanted you to feel happy here. *The Lord of the Rings* was always your favorite book."

"It's beautiful. But there's something I don't get: Why did I wake up in the room with the white walls? Why did no one talk to me? Why did I have to go to all that trouble to find out who I am?"

"You're in a tough place, Manuel. No one knows that better than me. So that you could hear the truth as gently as possible, you had to be able to take your fate in your own hands, at least to an extent. Instead of just telling you what happened, I wanted to give you the chance to find out for yourself. I didn't think you would do it this fast. I hope this shows you that your situation isn't hopeless."

"The idea that I have any control over my fate is just as much an illusion as this elf palace!" I mean to shout it, but my synthetic voice comes out flat.

"You can't see it like that," he argues. "Plenty of young men your age would give anything to be here and experience this fantasy world the way you can."

"And I would do anything to swap places with them."

"I understand, Manuel. But that's just not possible." He rests a hand on my shoulder but I can't feel it. "Why don't we go for a quick walk to check this place out? You'll see—the team put in a lot of work!"

CHAPTER 3

n terms of sensory impact, Elrond's palace is more real than the pictures of Hamburg projected onto the walls of the white room. The rooms are decorated with elaborate wood carvings and wall paintings, although the furniture is quite sparse. Elves wearing simple clothing bow, then rush past, as though they have important stuff to do.

"They're NPCs, I suppose?"

"I can see you haven't forgotten everything about gaming. No surprise, seeing how much time you spent playing them. Your mother wasn't too happy about that, but what could we do? I mean, I own a game company. But in answer to your question: Yes, they're all computer-controlled characters."

"Hey, you," I say to a pretty elf woman who's just walked through a door.

"Yes, sire?"

"What's the square root of six hundred and thirty?"

"Forgive me, sire, I'm just a simple serving girl and know

nothing of such things," the elf says in the same unnatural monotone as Alice.

"How old are you?"

"Forgive me, sire, I'm just a simple serving girl and know nothing of such things."

"They're not the sharpest tools in the box," I say.

"Of course, we can't fit all of the characters with high-spec artificial intelligence, that would blow our processing capacity," says the man, who as far as I know is my dad but still seems like a stranger to me. "There is someone I'd like you to meet, though. She's a little experimental, isn't in beta phase yet, but we're already quite proud of her capabilities." He waves over one of the elf servants. "Please bring Alandil."

"Yes, sire." The elf disappears into an adjoining room and comes back a short while later with a female elf wearing a plain olive-green dress. At first glance she doesn't look much different from the other NPCs, except her face has more detail and is less perfect, less masklike. She bows.

"You called, sire."

"This is Manuel. He will be our guest here for a time."

"It is a pleasure to meet you, Manuel." Alandil's voice is also simulated, but her intonation is more natural than that of the other simulated characters.

"What is the square root of six hundred and thirty?" I ask.

"Forgive me, sire, I'm just a simple serving girl and know nothing of such things."

I'm a little disappointed, but my father says: "Alandil doesn't know much about math, but is a skilled healer and knows all about elf history."

I'll bet. It's not that hard to program in a Tolkien dictionary or a few recipes for lotions and potions. I wonder how to test her supposed intelligence. Then I notice a vase standing on a side table. It's painted with scenes, like something from a fantasy novel.

I pick up the vase. It's easy to carry, just like the real thing, even though I can't feel its weight. I open a door onto a small room that might be an elf's living quarters, put the vase on the floor, then go back into the corridor.

"What's behind the door there?" I ask Alandil.

She looks at me for a second, as though she hasn't really understood the question. Just as I'm about to repeat it, she says: "You mean Gerfren's room?"

"Could be. What's inside the room?"

"Is this a game?" Alandil wants to know. At least that doesn't sound like a regular preprogrammed response.

"Yes."

She shuts her eyes, as though trying to concentrate. "In that room, there is a bed, a table, two chairs, a washbasin, two silver candelabras, a carved wooden chest, and the vase that you just carried in there."

Although I don't know much about how computer programs work, I'm stunned by her answer. I didn't expect a simulated person like Alandil to have such a clear image of the things inside the palace and be able to follow the consequences of my actions.

"Maybe you can to get to know each other better later," my father says. "I'd like to show you something else, Manuel."

"I shall return to work, then, sire, with your permission." Alandil bows gently. "It was a pleasure to meet you, Manuel. May I return the vase to its proper place?"

"Yes . . . yes, of course," I reply, amazed, and watch as she fetches the vase from the room and puts it back on the side table, smiles goodbye again, then disappears through another door. "She's awesome!"

"Right?" my father says.

"Can she really . . . think? Does she have awareness?"

"That's a tough one to answer. Not even philosophers, psychologists, neurologists, and computer scientists agree on what intelligence and awareness actually are. I've stopped trying to figure it out. For me, it's enough that, in most cases, Alandil behaves as though she is able to think. Come, there's something else I want to show you."

He leads me up a spiral staircase into a room that is dominated by a solitary, large table. A massive map is spread out on it. Although place names are written in what to me is illegible elf handwriting, I immediately recognize the distinctive rectangular outline of the mountain ranges that hide the dark kingdom of Mordor.

"What would you like to see first?" my father says.

"Are you saying this isn't just a simulation of Rivendell but the whole of Middle-earth too?"

"Yes. The Shire, Mirkwood, Rohan, Gondor, Isengard, Moria—we've got all the settings in the books. Of course, we're still working on certain areas, but there's already plenty to explore. I've put almost half of Dark Star's programmers, graphic artists, and designers on this, plus I've signed up two of the computer graphics experts that worked on the film of *The Hobbit*."

I stare at the map and take in all the fantasy places. Haven't I always dreamed of seeing them for myself? That's what it feels like, but I don't remember. But now that I actually have the chance, I can't decide where to start. Maybe it would be easiest to go from the beginning of the book.

"I'd like to go to Hobbiton."

"All right."

I expect us to teleport straight there, but my father signals at me to follow. We go down corridors, climb a steep winding staircase, and finally reach a sort of roof terrace that must be at the top of the palace. From here, there's a good view of the whole region nestling perfectly in the valley's natural contour, as though it had grown out of the rock.

"What are we doing here?" I ask.

"At first, I thought you could move around by magic," he explains. "But the team thought that wouldn't work well, that for this world to actually seem real you'd have to get to know its limitations too. I mean, not even Gandalf can teleport from place to place. But I honestly thought if you had to spend ages traveling you'd get bored. So in the end we agreed on this."

He pulls a sort of flute from his clothing and plays a short tune. A shrill cry comes in response. It seems to come from far away, and a short while later two black outlines appear over the mountains and quickly approach until I can make out that they are giant eagles. They flap their wings forcefully and land next to us on the terrace. The air current ruffles my father's hair and flaps his clothing, but I feel nothing.

My father climbs onto the back of one of the giant birds and I do the same. The eagles flap their wings, take off, and rise in circles, as though carried by an invisible wind. Soon, we have a view over the peaks of the surrounding mountain ranges.

It's an incredible feeling to glide over Rivendell on the back of an eagle. I have to remind myself it's just an illusion. As I gaze down over the edge of the feathered neck, I'm overcome by a wave of vertigo and involuntarily clutch tighter.

The simulated world seems endless. I see rivers, forests, and distant mountain ranges stretching into the horizon. The landscape only blurs a little as it gets further away.

"To Hobbiton!" my father yells, and, judging from his voice, he's having fun.

According to the map, the distance between Rivendell and the Shire isn't great, but it still takes a while before the birds glide down through a hilly landscape and land in the middle of the hobbit village. Dozens of small inhabitants immediately rush out of their mud huts and surround us, amazed. Small children point at us. The illusion of sudden excitement intruding into usually calm village life is almost pitch perfect.

I climb off the bird. My father gets off his eagle too and both creatures disappear into the clouds. The hobbits stare at us expectantly, as though they're waiting for my instructions.

I could be a hero in this world, a king, maybe even a god. The idea is tempting . . . and yet suddenly I see the excitedly chatting hobbits for what they really are: lifeless puppets with no free will, no real feelings, no soul. Without knowing why, I suddenly feel repelled by the fact that they seem so real. I have a vague but overwhelming sense that I shouldn't be here.

"I want to go back to the white room."

"But why, son? Don't you like it here?"

"I do. I'm just not in the mood for gaming."

"You think this is just a computer game?" His disappointment is obvious. "Do you have any idea how much work went into all of this? We created this world for you. It's almost limitless. You'll never get bored here. You can have adventures, explore the depths of Moria, or battle giant spiders, if you want. You can command an entire army and challenge the Dark Lord!"

"But it's not real," I argue.

"I know it still feels strange to you, but you'll get used to it. At some point you'll forget this isn't real. Our brain is built so that it adapts to the most unusual circumstances and at some point accepts them as normal. Unlike me and everyone else out there, you'll never feel pain, hunger, thirst. If you die during an adventure, that's just a temporary setback. And if you want, we can invite other people here. We could open bits of Middle-earth to the public, like multiplayer games. That way you could meet people from all over the world and make new friends. At the same time, you'd be the most powerful being in this world, with more magic than Gandalf or Sauron, if that's what you want."

"I'm sorry. It's really great here, but . . . it's a fantasy world. I already feel as though I don't exist. I think I want to stick as close to reality as possible. At least until I remember my life from before."

"I understand," my father says sadly. "This must all be very hard on you." He points at the hobbit village. "All right, none of this is going anywhere. You can come back anytime. Just tell me when you're in the mood. I . . . just have to take care of a couple of things. We'll speak later."

Before I can say goodbye, I'm alone again in the room with the white glowing walls.

CHAPTER 4

"Alice, show me Maria Jaspers!"

A load of internet articles and pictures fill the four walls of my room. She was beautiful: slim, with dark, curly hair that I must have inherited from her. In most of the pictures she's wearing fancy clothes at benefits, the Berlinale, and rich people's parties. The articles that aren't about her death are all from around the time she married my father. There's one from 2006 that's about how they met: my father had a skiing accident and my mother was working as a nurse at the Innsbruck hospital where he was treated. It was 1996, just after he'd graduated with a degree in business studies. A picture shows a cheerful, curly-haired child sitting next to her on the floor, playing with a Game Boy. Is that really me? I use my virtual hand to swipe across the wall, zoom in on pictures, left click, open more articles. Nothing I'm reading triggers any memories. She's like a stranger. And I'm almost angrier about that than I am about the way she died: her killers stole my memories of her.

"She was an incredible woman."

I don't know how long my father's virtual figure has been standing there. Anyway, there was nothing—no sound, flash, or anything else—to give away that he'd arrived.

I want to say: Yes, she was. But that would feel like a lie, because I don't know anything about her. I don't even know her voice.

"Open securecloudstorage.com, slash hjaspers, slash photos," my father says.

The internet pictures disappear and are replaced by folder icons. One is labeled "Manuel," another "Maria." He clicks open a folder with pictures of my mother. Now I see her home life: playing with her young child, cooking, opening Christmas presents. There are even a couple of her in the shower, hiding behind the curtain, half smiling, half indignant.

My father clicks open a video. It's from a trip to an amusement park at Lüneburg Heath. I must be around three years old and I'm cowering behind her legs, scared of a giant cuddly bear. Later, I'm sitting on a carousel, waving at her and my father, who must be holding the camera. In the next scene, I'm holding a massive ice cream and my face is covered in goo. I drop the cone and start to cry. My mother tries to comfort me and wipes sticky ice cream off my clothes. She turns to my father and scolds: "You could help instead of just standing there filming everything!" And with that, the film ends.

They're the first words I've heard her say. At least, as far as I remember. Her voice is alien to me. I want to cry like the kid in the film, the one that must have been me but feels like someone else.

My father can cry. I hear him sobbing and sniffing, though the avatar standing next to me doesn't move or show any feelings.

"Thanks for showing me that," I say. He doesn't answer. "Tell me about her."

"She . . . she was amazing. Mostly gentle, but she had a real temper when she got upset. Once she threw a milk carton at my head. Then I had to clean up because in her mind it was my fault for setting her off. That's what she was like: stubborn, uncompromising, determined. It was just like her to confront the men that broke into the house. And she would rather die than ever let them get you. I've never loved anyone the way I love her. She loved me too, of course, but you were more important than anything. I always had to stop her from being overprotective. If ever a teacher dared give you a low grade, well, he'd be in for it. But that almost never happened—you were always a really good, hardworking pupil."

"Do I have any brothers and sisters?"

"No. Your birth was . . . complicated. You were in neonatal intensive care for a while, but luckily there was no lasting damage. Your mother couldn't have any more children after that. I think that just made her love you more."

"Where's she buried?"

"At the Ohlsdorf Cemetery."

"Can I . . . can I see her grave?"

"We can do that. But first, I have something else I want to show you. Or do you need a rest first? I imagine this is all quite confusing and exhausting."

"It is. But I'd like to see what it is you want to show me."

"Good. Alice, show private camera C-113!"

The photos disappear. All the walls are white, except one. It shows a basement that looks a bit like a gym, with exercise mats on the floor and strip lighting. The camera shakes gently. It's strapped to someone's head.

My father's avatar is gone but I can hear his voice: "Can you see where I am?"

"I see a basement with exercise mats."

"Exactly. You're looking through my glasses. It's like I'm carrying you piggyback." He looks around again, slowly. That way I get to check out the whole room. But there's nothing interesting other than some gym equipment and a stand with a VR headset and cybergloves.

"I'm not wearing the gloves now, so I'm using voice control and this thing." His hand appears, holding a smartphone.

He opens a door, walks into a strip-lit basement corridor, then down another corridor until he reaches a big garage. There's a red Ferrari and a big black SUV with tinted windows. My father gets into the SUV.

"Henning Jaspers," he says.

"Identification successful. Welcome, Henning Jaspers," a computer voice replies.

"Drive out of the garage!"

The engine starts. It gets lighter as the garage door opens and the car drives out. My father isn't even touching the steering wheel.

"Do you see, Manuel?"

"Yes . . . Father." The word feels strange to say.

"You used to call me Dad." He sounds a little hurt.

"Yes, Dad."

"So, this is a self-drive car. It can take you anywhere you want to go—totally on autopilot. They're not officially approved for road use in Germany yet, but I have a special permit for test drives. You can take it anywhere you like."

I'm stunned. "Me?"

"Yes. Watch, it's really easy. Just tell Alice: 'Taking over mobile steering one.' Or you can say 'ME-1.'"

"Taking over ME-1."

A picture comes up on another wall that shows the view from my father's glasses but from a little higher up. The camera must be attached to the car roof. I see a garage under a wide, modern villa. A simple command menu sits at the bottom of the picture. Arrows point forward, left, and right. There's a blank field labeled DESTINATION.

"Click on the 'Destination' field and say 'Ohlsdorf Cemetery.'"

I do as he says. The car's computer confirms the destination. I watch through the camera as the car drives up a broad ramp and turns onto a quiet, residential street. The car drives through traffic, maintains braking distance, stays within the speed limit, and obeys road signals and red lights, just like a learner driver taking his test. My father and I don't have to lift a finger. A map showing the car's location appears in the corner of the screen. Small camera images show the view from behind and to the sides.

"Excellent!" my father says. "Do you see the arrows at the bottom of the picture? You can use them to direct the car if you want to take a different route. Move the arrow to the right."

I activate the arrow and it flashes red. The car turns right at the next junction even though the GPS was going to take us left. Twice more, my father lets me take a different route to Ohlsdorf than the one set by the GPS.

"Well done. Now double click on the right arrow. The car will find the next right turn to get off the road, by turning into a driveway, a parking place, a garage, or, in this case, a country track."

The car turns onto a narrow path and after about a hundred yards reaches a clearing that's a parking area and set-off point for weekend hikers.

"Now press the stop button!" The car comes to a standstill. "There's one more surprise in the back." He turns in his seat and points at a partition sectioning off the car trunk. It's impossible to see what's back there. "Tell Alice: 'Activate ME-4.'"

I give the command and another picture appears on the third wall of my room, but this one's black. At the bottom, there are controls like the car controls, but more complicated. My father tells me which command to give next.

"Alice, start ME-4!" I say.

A loud buzzing sound fills the white room and the picture

from the car roof camera shudders gently. Suddenly the picture on the third wall lights up, but I still can't make anything out. Then the camera moves up and I see a light about six feet above the car-roof camera.

"A drone!"

"Exactly! It should be able to get you most places you can't reach by car. Its battery runs for around twenty minutes' flight time. It'll automatically fly back to the charging station in the car when it's running out of power."

He explains how to operate the height, speed, flight, and camera view. The camera can even project a panoramic picture onto the four walls, ceiling, and floor of my room.

I use the drone to glide over the forest for a while. A dog walker looks up, annoyed. Even though I'm only experiencing the outside world through a virtual video projection, for the first time since waking up in this simulated environment, I feel free. The drone is easy to control and surprisingly fast. My father says it can fly to a height of five hundred yards, but I stick close to the forest canopy because I don't want to mess up Hamburg Airport's flight safety.

"You should head back to the car now, Manuel. Just click on the 'home' button and the drone will fly back automatically."

I'm still in panoramic mode and see my father standing in the clearing next to the car. He waves. The drone drops through the open roof into its stand in the car trunk, then turns itself off. The view from the car camera and my father's glasses reappears.

"Wow!" I yell. "That was amazing! Thanks, Dad!"

"I'm really pleased you like it. You may not be able to use your body, but this means you're not completely cut off from the real world. Actually, you can probably get around more easily and faster than most people."

"So, I'm like a human brain trapped in a robot body," I say with a hint of sarcasm.

"If you like. But a robot body is still better than no body, don't you think?"

"True. Thanks, Dad. Thanks for everything!"

"The least I can do after what happened is give you a halfway decent life. What those cowards . . . I would give anything to undo what happened. So that your mother could be here with us, hold you the way she . . . the way she used to." He sounds like he's holding back tears.

"Let's drive to her grave."

"Yes, son."

He gets back into the car, but this time sits in the passenger seat. I take over the controls and let the GPS select the route. Every time we stop at a red light, I look through my father's glasses at the people standing on the sidewalk or sitting in cars alongside us, pointing in amazement. The car has tinted windows but they can still tell no one is at the wheel. Despite causing a sensation, we reach the large parking lot at the edge of the Ohlsdorf Cemetery without incident.

My father walks the rest of the way, past small cemetery

chapels and gravestones, some of which are hundreds of years old, shadowed by beech, oak, and chestnut trees.

My mother's gravestone is simple but set apart in a small clearing. It can only be reached down a narrow path bordered by lush rhododendron bushes—their white, lilac, and blue flowers glow as though her grave is giving off a special life force that has power over nature.

Maria Jaspers, née Hochleitner. 9.26.1970–8.30.2016

Nothing else is written on the gray granite gravestone. There's not even a cross or any other kind of religious symbol.

"Your mother wasn't really a churchgoer," my father says, as though reading my mind. "To be honest, I don't believe in an afterlife or an all-powerful creator any more than she did."

"What did she believe in?" I ask.

"Love," my father says. "She believed that love is everlasting, that it transcends death. She was convinced that the more you love and are loved, the more value your life has, and she believed that love survives long after the body has gone. And she was right."

We're silent as his words run through me. But I don't feel her love for me, or my love for her—just endless anger.

CHAPTER 5

"Do the police have any suspects?" I say, hating how blank my voice sounds.

"Hundreds. But they don't have any leads yet."

"You mean the police have nothing? After eight months of investigations?"

"I wouldn't put it like that. I phone Chief Inspector Krüger regularly. He thinks a criminal organization is behind this, and that they wanted to kidnap you to get money out of me."

"Can't it have been regular burglars?"

"No. They had to turn off the security systems before breaking in. From outside, by hacking in. Otherwise the security team would have been alerted. I thought the system was secure, but they found a weakness. The whole thing must have been planned well in advance. That's why the police think the intruders wanted ransom money. Your mother stopped them from taking you—but she paid with her life."

"Is there any CCTV footage?"

"No, unfortunately not."

"But there must be something, some clue as to how it happened."

"Of course. The forensics team spent a whole day at the house. The police are following up on even the tiniest leads . . . but we can talk about it more tomorrow. Let's go home."

As he turns onto the main path, a slim woman with long black hair walks toward us. Her snow-white dress doesn't fit in the cemetery. My father watches her go by, then she turns and looks at him. I don't know why, but I suddenly feel she isn't looking at him, but at me. As though she knows I can see her through the camera glasses. A second later my father turns to look straight ahead and she disappears from my line of vision.

"Did you recognize that woman?" I ask.

"What woman?"

"The woman in white who just walked past."

"I don't know what you mean."

I let it drop. He probably just turned to look, the way men often do when they see an attractive woman, and now he's embarrassed. The idea that she was looking at me is probably nothing more than my overwrought senses playing tricks on me.

"You should try to sleep," my father says, getting back into the car.

"How? My virtual room has no bed."

"Just say 'good night' to Alice."

I try it and the video stream disappears. The walls turn white, then yellowish, and the light slowly fades until I'm surrounded by darkness. I start to panic, suddenly feeling as though I'm in a grave, like my mother. The fear gradually subsides. I try to remember her: her touch, her voice, her smell. But there's nothing. It's as though I've only ever existed inside this room.

The light comes back on.

"Good morning, Manuel," says Alice in her neutral monotone.

"What?" I ask, confused. "Did I sleep?" I don't remember any of my dreams.

"You slept for twelve hours and fifty-three minutes," the computer tells me. "It is now eight thirteen a.m."

The pain and anger I felt yesterday at my mother's graveside are still there. I decide to find out who killed her. There's not much chance of success, but it's not as though I have anything better to do. Plus it'll help take my mind off how bleak it all is—at least, that's what I hope.

"Alice, I would like to talk to my father."

"Henning Jaspers is busy at the moment. Would you like to leave a message?"

"Yes."

"Please speak after the tone." There is a beep.

"Hi, Dad, this is Manuel. Please get in touch when you have time. I'd like to find out more about how Mom . . . died. Later. End of message."

"The message has been saved."

I decide to find out more by myself, while I'm waiting for him to get in touch. "Alice, what do you know about the murder of Maria Jaspers?"

"I don't understand the question."

"Show me the murder of Maria Jaspers."

The walls fill with pictures and articles from the internet. It's mostly the same stuff I saw yesterday. MURDER OF MILLIONAIRE'S WIFE REMAINS A MYSTERY, a headline reads. The article is just as uninformative as the headline.

There's no way around it—I need my father to get answers. I kill time by watching people on Eyestream; I jog with Elena96 along the riverbank for a while. Someone with the username Wildworldwatcher sits stock-still somewhere in the African bush, watching lions tear apart a zebra. ChantalB stands in a queue outside the Eiffel Tower. It's a little after midnight in Los Angeles, and I follow a young man into a fashionable nightclub. It's all pretty cool, but feels like a waste of time, so I'm glad when my father's avatar finally appears in my room.

He looks at the video images on the walls. "Ah, Eyestream. You're joining in with other people's lives. That's great. That's really great, son."

"Except it isn't my life. I'm just a spectator."

"Of course. I know that. Which is why I had the car and drone made. So you could at least move around freely. And you can travel around the world with these people too. The only thing is, I don't want you to contact anyone through the internet. No one must find out you're awake."

"Why not?"

"What we've done here, implanting electrodes into your head, this virtual world, the internet access, your simulated voice, all of it would attract a huge amount of interest," he says, his voice becoming urgent. "If the press gets wind of this, neither of us will ever get another moment's peace. The world would expect us to cure the blind and mute, bring patients out of comas, and who knows what else. We'd be swamped by desperate begging letters. The pressure would be huge and I wouldn't be able to focus on you anymore."

"Would it be so bad to help other people?"

"We're just not there yet. Some people will think all this is immoral or unethical or unchristian or whatever. People are always scared of new things. Manuel, over the last few months I've done everything to save you, even though I couldn't help your mother . . . I'm just not ready to bring this into the public domain. Please promise you won't tell anyone about this. For now, at least. We can discuss it again in a few weeks' time."

"All right, got it," I concede. There are more urgent questions on my mind than keeping silent about my treatment.

"Thanks. I'm counting on you," he says, relieved. "So you wanted to talk about your mother?"

"Yes. I'd like to know more about how Mom died."

His voice becomes flat. "She was already dead when I found her. Her body was lying across your bed. There was blood everywhere.

- 43 -

We found a can of pepper spray on the floor with her fingerprints on it, but later the police couldn't find any traces of it in the air. That means she didn't get a chance to use it. From the forensic evidence it looks as though at least two intruders went into your room. The police only found that out later too."

So I must have been awake when they came into my room. Was I scared? Did I yell, or cower under my duvet while she struggled to save me? Why can't I remember anything?

"My memories of that night are vague," he says. "I was in shock. I woke up because I heard shouting. Then there were two shots. The first one grazed her and hit you in the neck, the second got her in the head, and she died instantly. I ran into your room but the intruders had already left. I activated the alarm and that automatically called the ambulance and police. I thought you were dead."

"But why would they kill her? They can't have been scared of a can of pepper spray?"

"If you ever get your memory back, you'll know your mother could be pretty scary when she got angry. Maybe the first shot was fired as a reflex, because the intruder was caught off guard. The second shot, the one that killed her, was probably fired so she wouldn't be able to give evidence. Then they ran away."

"How can the police ever identify the intruders without forensic evidence?"

"Please don't worry about all this, Manuel. I know it's a lot to get your head around. But there's nothing to be done."

I ignore his request. "What if it wasn't a kidnapping? Maybe the intruders wanted to kill us both."

"There's nothing to suggest that. But, sure, the police are looking at that too."

"Maybe you know one of the intruders?"

"What makes you say that?"

"You said someone hacked into the security system. Maybe it was security staff. Or someone around you who knew the system."

"Manuel, please believe me, the police have already been through this," my father says, getting annoyed. "They've looked into everyone who had anything to do with the security system."

But I can't let it go. "Maybe it's someone that worked at your company? You own Dark Star Game Studios. There must be loads of people there with the technical expertise. Can you think of anyone with a grudge against you? Maybe someone you fell out with? Or someone that got fired?"

"Manuel, this won't get you anywhere! You're a fifteen-year-old boy and have no police experience. You're really smart, sure, but that's not enough to help you find something the police haven't already been able to find. It's sad, I get that, but you can't help bring the people that killed your mother to justice. Even though I understand why you want to."

No, there's no way he could understand. I feel like crying, but my virtual body can't make tears and my computer voice can't sob.

CHAPTER 6

After my father leaves, I keep trawling the internet for information about my mother's murder, but the news reports don't tell me anything new. I read articles about the abductions of millionaire kids, like Richard Oetker, Sabine and Susanne Kronzucker, Lars and Meike Schlecker. The kidnappers were always totally ruthless and meticulous, but other than that those cases are nothing like mine. I feel helpless. Useless. My father's right: I can't get justice.

A few hours later my father's avatar reappears. But this time he isn't alone: a rugged-looking man in jeans and a T-shirt is next to him. The newcomer looks around as though he has no idea how he got here.

"This is Pieter de Boor," my father explains. "He's one of the people I hired to protect you."

"Hey!" the man says.

"Hello," I reply. "To protect me? How do you mean?"

"Someone shot you. It's unlikely that person wanted to kill

you, but I can't take any risks. The room your body is in is guarded 24/7."

I shudder at the idea that someone might want to kill me. Why would anyone want to do that?

"Like I said, it's unlikely anyone is after you," my father says, probably picking up on my alarm. "Don't worry. You're safe. That's one of the advantages of living in a virtual world: Nothing can touch you. No car accident, no terrorist attack, no natural disaster."

"I'd be happy to deal with those threats if it meant being free."

"I know. That's why I asked Pieter here. When I saw that you like following people on Eyestream, I had an idea. Alice, open Pietercam."

Pieter's avatar disappears. Instead, a camera image is projected onto a wall. It shows the basement room my father uses when he's moving around the virtual world. He's there, wearing a VR headset and cybergloves.

"Pieter, please stand in front of the mirror," my father says. The camera moves and I see a man's reflection. He's wearing jeans and a dark polo shirt that outlines a muscular torso. His head is clean-shaven and he has a blond goatee. Steely blue eyes stare at me through the camera glasses. His smile is a little creepy.

"Hey, Manuel. Can you see me?" He has a strong Dutch accent.

"Yes, I can see you."

"Excellent," my father says. "So Pieter's what you could call your avatar in the real world. He'll do whatever you say so long as it isn't illegal or dangerous."

"I . . . am . . . a . . . ro-bot," Pieter rasps, making a few jerky movements in front of the mirror. I can't help laughing. My computer voice sounds really weird when I do.

"I can see you're going to get along," my father says. "You'll have a great time, I'm sure."

Pieter seems nice. I like the idea that we'll be a team. Then again, it feels a little strange to boss someone around.

"Pieter, can you show me around the house, please?"

"You bet, boss!" he says with a hint of irony.

He leaves the basement and takes me through the house. It has two separate block-shaped wings that connect through a circular area in the middle. In the basement, next to the gym used for trips into the virtual world, there's a swimming pool, sauna, boiler room, wine cellar, a closed-off security room, and a big garage. Next to the semicircular entrance hall on the ground floor there's a modern kitchen with a pantry; a big dining room; and a living room with a curved panoramic window onto the parklike garden; there's my father's study, with bookshelves; two guest rooms; and a room with a brick fireplace, billiard table, and large conference table. The top floor includes my parents' room and my room. It's all modern, and simply but tastefully decorated. Is that my mother's touch?

Pieter gives a running commentary, like a guide showing tourists around the palace of an ancient king. I like the self-deprecation.

"And you really don't remember any of this?" he says at one point.

"No. It's like I'm here for the first time."

"That must be bad. Not having a past."

"It is bad," I say in my completely blank voice. "What about your past? What did you do before you worked for my father?"

"I was in the army. I'm from Cape Town and served in the South African forces. After that I was with a private security firm, working on contracts for foreign companies. Sometimes I had the impression I was working for the Secret Service but, of course, we were never told who our actual client was."

"Sounds exciting."

"It's a dirty business. I'm glad I don't have to do that anymore."

"Have you ever killed anyone?"

He's quiet for a moment. When he answers, I can tell he's holding his anger in check: "Never ask me that again, okay?"

"S-sorry, Pieter. I didn't mean to upset you."

"It's all right. There are just some things I don't like to talk about."

"Sorry. I'll never ask again."

"I'm going to clock off now. You can contact me any time after eight in the morning if you need to. Good night, Manuel."

"Good night, Pieter. Alice, close Pietercam."

It's still early and I'm not tired. I have nothing better to do so scroll through the Eyestreams currently active in Hamburg. I find a stream from someone called LittleDevil having a barbecue in City Park with a few friends. A young man with a beard and ponytail is playing the guitar and singing while everyone around him listens attentively. Although he isn't particularly talented, I feel moved. Have I ever played the guitar? What I would give to do that now! Maybe tomorrow I can ask Pieter if he plays any musical instruments. Though that wouldn't be the same.

One of the girls stands up and heads to a crate of beer near the barbecue. She picks up a bottle, opens it, and turns to face the woman with the camera glasses. "Want one?" I freeze. I know this girl! The black hair, the eyes that are a little too big for her face, the narrow chin ... I don't remember her name but am 100 percent sure I've seen her before. For the first time since waking up in the white room, I feel connected to something in the outside world. The girl means something to me, but I don't know *what*.

I promised my father I wouldn't contact anyone, but this is too important. I don't have to say I'm a young guy in a coma able to surf the internet thanks to electrode implants in my brain. I use Alice to dictate a chat message to LittleDevil: *Who is the girl with the black hair that just got herself a beer?*

"Hey, Julia, someone wants to know who you are!" says the woman with the camera glasses.

"You mean the camera's on?" Julia says. The others turn to look at LittleDevil.

The guitarist stops playing. "Switch that damned thing off! I don't feel like playing a concert for the NSA!"

"Sorry, I—" the girl with the glasses begins, and the picture goes black. A message tells me that LittleDevil is offline.

Damn!

I do a Google picture search. It finds loads of Julias in Hamburg but none who look like the girl in City Park. Why didn't I think to take a screenshot?

I ask Alice to contact my father. This time I only hear his voice. His picture is projected onto one of the walls in my room, but it's not a video link. It looks like it's a Dark Star Game Studios press photo.

"Hi, Manuel," he says. "I was about to go to bed."

"Sorry to bother you . . ."

"No, I didn't mean it like that, son. You're never a bother! How did it go with Pieter?"

"Good. Thanks for arranging the camera. It's really kind."

"I'm glad you get along."

"It's something else. I was just on Eyestream and saw a girl. I think I know her from somewhere."

"A girl? What's her name?"

"I just know her first name: Julia."

"Hmm. And you can't remember where you know her from?"

"No."

"School maybe?"

"Could be. What school did I go to?"

"Walddörfer High School."

"Thanks, Dad. Good night!"

"You're welcome. It's good you're starting to remember things. You'll probably get your memory back soon. Good night, son!"

I'm too wired to sleep, so I check out the high school website and look through a few social media sites for any Julias who go to the school. I find quite a few but their profile pictures look different from the girl in City Park.

It's way past midnight by the time I give up. "Good night, Alice."

The light turns off and I'm surrounded by darkness. This time it doesn't scare me.

CHAPTER 7

A little before eight, the walls of the white room get brighter and I hear Alice's synthetic voice give her morning greeting: "Good morning, Manuel."

Snatches of a weird dream drift through my mind. Julia was there. She'd been captured by orcs and taken to a tower. I had to free her, but for some reason I couldn't find a way in. Suddenly, the orcs took me prisoner. They were laughing, jeering at me, and Julia was sitting outside my cell crying. All I can read into the dream is that this girl must mean something to me. Were we boyfriend and girlfriend? But then, wouldn't my father have known her?

I decide to send a message to LittleDevil and ask about Julia. Even though I promised my father I wouldn't contact anyone, the upside of the internet is that you can be anonymous.

Hello, LittleDevil, I dictate into Eyestream Chat. *I saw a girl on your stream yesterday—Julia. I know her but don't have her contact details. Can you tell me how to reach her?*

The status on LittleDevil's profile says she is offline, but I get a reply almost immediately: *What's your name? How do you know Julia?*

I hesitate. I'd planned to stay anonymous, but she won't tell me anything about Julia unless I give her something. *My name is Manuel. I'm not sure how I know her.*

I don't have to wait long for a reply: *What does that mean? "I'm not sure how I know her"? Either you know her or you don't, "Manuel."*

I don't even hesitate. I decide to take another risk. *I was in an accident. I don't remember anything about my life. I just know that I've met Julia. Maybe she can help me get my memory back. Please, it's really important that I talk to her.*

That's the dumbest story I ever heard! LittleDevil replies. *Piss off, stalker!*

It's not like that, I write back. *Please ask Julia if she knows a 15-year-old guy called Manuel who has dark brown curly hair. She can decide for herself whether or not to contact me.*

But the message doesn't reach LittleDevil. Eyestream says she's blocked me.

I delete my account and open another one using a different username. Then I subscribe to LittleDevil's stream and set things up so that Eyestream will send me a notification when she's back online. I have nothing better to do with my endless free time, so randomly click through other streams in Hamburg. I'm not likely to accidentally find Julia or anyone else from my earlier life, but maybe I'll see something that triggers a memory. Either way, it's better than just staring at a blank wall.

Two hours later I've had enough of shaky camera footage. I've been following a Chinese tourist giving his invisible audience a running commentary as he walks through the market outside city hall. I should stop. Enough is enough.

Then I see her: the woman in the snow-white dress.

She turns her head and seems to smile right at me as she passes by, disappearing out of the frame. The Chinese man chats on in his hard-to-understand singsong accent.

Was that really the woman from the cemetery? Even if it was her—even if seeing her on Eyestream was some weird coincidence—it doesn't mean anything. It *can't* mean anything. She was smiling at the Chinese man, or someone else, not me. She probably didn't even know he was recording the scene on camera. That's the only explanation.

And yet . . .

An idea comes to me: What if I didn't actually see her? What if I just projected her face onto some other passerby who happened to be wearing a white dress, the way you sometimes see a shape in an inkblot or a cloud? But if that's true, whose face is it?

"Alice, show me Maria Jaspers."

All the pictures and online reports that I've already looked through pop up again. She does look a little like the woman in white—long dark hair, slim—but her face is different. Her nose is thinner, her lips a little fuller. No, if I did actually project a familiar face onto the face of a stranger, it wasn't my mother's.

A notification from Eyestream pops up: LittleDevil is online. I open her stream and follow LittleDevil and a redheaded woman with freckles as they wander through a shopping center. They stare into shopwindows and laugh at what other people are wearing. I try to think of a way to contact her without getting myself blocked.

They stop outside a clothes shop and I have an idea. I open Google Maps and type in the name of the place. It's in the Alstertal shopping center.

"Alice, contact Pieter!"

"Hey, boss," the South African says. "What can I do for you?"

I hesitate. Is my idea really such a good plan? After all, Pieter works for my father, who expressly told me not to contact anyone on the outside. But then, the South African doesn't seem too bothered by rules and it's the best plan I've got. It's worth a chance, anyway.

"Could you please go to the Alstertal shopping center?"

"What for? You want to go shopping?"

"No, but there's someone there I'd like you to track for me."

"Sounds fun. Okay, I'm on my way."

I project the view from Pieter's camera on to one wall and follow LittleDevil on Eyestream on another, hoping she doesn't turn her camera off. Luckily for me, the two young women just keep chatting. They're standing in front of a window full of summer clothes when Pieter pulls into the shopping center parking lot.

"That's really pretty," LittleDevil says, pointing at a lime-green dress.

"Not sure," her friend says. "Bit loud, maybe."

"You think?"

"Now what, boss?" Pieter asks.

I give him the name of the shop. While he's trying to find it, the girls go inside. LittleDevil looks for the dress in her size and takes it into the fitting room. I catch her reflection in the mirror. She's tall and slim with short blonde hair, in her early twenties. Her hand goes up to the glasses and the picture turns black. LittleDevil is offline. Crap! Pieter arrives at the shop a few minutes later. His camera shows the girls leaving the shop.

"What now, boss?" he says.

LittleDevil glances at him, but luckily her friend drags her away. I catch bits of their conversation:

"No way . . . especially not at that price . . ."

"Pieter, the two women that just came out of the shop," I say, "I need to talk to one of them. The blonde one with the plastic bag."

He turns so that I can see them through his camera. "What do you want to say?"

He walks a few steps behind them while I explain. They go into a café and sit at a table.

Pieter takes his own approach. "Excuse me, ladies." They look up at him. LittleDevil frowns, cautious, but her friend smiles. She seems to like Pieter.

"What do you want?" LittleDevil asks.

"Can I get you a coffee?"

The redhead likes the idea but LittleDevil is dismissive. "No thanks, we'd rather be on our own. And next time you want to hit on us, turn your camera glasses off."

"Sorry, but that's the whole point. You could say that I brought someone with me, a good friend. He'd like to talk to you."

"So why doesn't he just come here himself?"

"Because he can't."

"What does that even mean? Is he disabled, or what?"

The camera picture moves up and down as Pieter nods.

She seems embarrassed at his answer and her voice softens a little: "So what does your friend want?"

"He wants to get in touch with a girl called Julia, someone you know."

"The nutjob off the internet!" LittleDevil is annoyed. "You've got to be joking! He's following me again? Eyestream's a bad idea."

"He's not a nutjob," Pieter explains. "Not even a bit. He was in an accident and lost his memory. He thinks he knows Julia from before. If he could talk to her it might help him get better."

"That story again! How do I even know it's true? Maybe you're the nutjob and made the whole thing up yourself."

"Do I look like a nutjob?"

"What if it's true?" the redhead asks.

"And what if it isn't?" LittleDevil says. "I'm not giving Julia's address to a total stranger."

"Okay, I get it. How much do you want?" Pieter says.

"What?" The redhead is shocked. LittleDevil scowls.

"I really want to help Manuel," Pieter explains. "So, how much do you want?" I can't believe what I'm seeing. He puts two €50 bills on the table. I didn't ask him to bribe LittleDevil and feel really uncomfortable about this, but it's done now.

The Eyestreamer touches the money, thinking. Her friend looks horrified. "Two hundred," LittleDevil says.

Pieter puts another two fifties on the table.

"Good," she says, pocketing the cash. "Her Nymochat name is July2001. That's all I'm telling you."

Somehow it doesn't feel right to use information that's been bought, but if I want to get my memory back I can't be too coy about things. I don't know Nymochat but Google links me to a website that claims to be a "totally anonymous chat site." It still has user profiles. July2001's picture is a blue unicorn—there's nothing else. No way for me to know whether the profile actually belongs to Julia. But I don't want to keep asking questions.

"Okay, that'll do."

Pieter turns and leaves LittleDevil and her friend. "Do you still need me? Otherwise I'll do a bit of shopping while I'm here."

"No, that's okay. I'll be in touch. Thanks, Pieter. That was a big help."

"No problem. Later, boss."

"See you, Pieter. Alice, close Pietercam."

I register a Nymochat account under "Boy in a White Room."

I feel nervous, and struggle to find the right words to explain my situation to July2001:

Hello Julia,

My name is Manuel. I saw you in City Park through Eyestream. There was a guy playing the guitar. I think I know you but don't know where from. I lost my memory in an accident. I am fifteen years old and have dark, curly hair. I don't have a picture of myself. If we know each other please tell me where from—it could help me remember my former life.

Manuel

I'm not expecting a quick answer, but just seconds later I get a jolt when a message appears in my Nymochat account. It reads: *If this is a joke, then it's not funny.*

It's not a joke, I write. *I can't tell you anything else. Not yet. Just that I'm Manuel and can't remember anything about my life, except that I know you.*

Manuel? How's this even possible? Where are you?

Before I tell you where I am, I need to know how we know each other, I answer.

How we know each other? If you're really who you say you are then how could you not know? I'm your sister!

CHAPTER 8

stare at the screen, stunned. My Nymochat account is gone and all that's showing is an error message: "Connection terminated."

"Alice, what happened?"

"I don't understand the question."

"Why has the Nymochat connection shut down?"

"I don't understand the question."

"Alice, open Nymochat."

"There is a technical error. Please wait."

A technical error? Now?

"Alice, contact my father."

His face is big on the screen and there are bookshelves in the background. He must be talking from a webcam in his office.

"Hello, son. You wanted to chat?"

I get straight to the point. "Do I have a sister?"

"What makes you say that?" he says, frowning.

"Please answer the question first. Do I have a sister called Julia?"

"No, of course not. I already said your mother couldn't have any more kids after you were born. Where did you get that idea?"

I tell him how I first saw Julia, how seeing her triggered something, like someone tugging a thread, how I got in touch with her and that the connection broke.

"Manuel, we agreed you wouldn't talk to anyone," he says, more gentle than angry.

"I know. But I thought finding her would help me get my memory back more quickly."

"Well, whoever this Julia person is, she isn't your sister. I can tell you that much."

"Why would she say she is, then?"

"She said that? Before answering, think carefully about what she said."

"She said if I am who I say I am, then she's my sister."

"But maybe you aren't who she thought you were. Maybe she really does have a brother called Manuel. Maybe he's around your age with dark, curly hair. They're not exactly uncommon characteristics. You didn't show her a picture of yourself, did you?"

"No."

"At least you had the sense not to do that. I already told you how dangerous it is to reveal your identity. Manuel, what happened today must never happen again. I'll have to talk to Pieter."

"It can't just be a coincidence! I recognize her and she happens to know a Manuel who happens to be my age!"

"Well, that's what she says. Are you certain that the girl on

Nymochat really is the Julia you saw on Eyestream? It could just be the two girls from the shopping center trying to use you—or me, to be more accurate. Something along the lines of: *It'll probably be easy to get even more cash out of someone willing to pay two hundred euros for a Nymochat username.* Maybe they even suspect who you are. Can you see where all this might lead?"

"But I recognize her! I'm sure I know Julia from before!"

"Manuel, sometimes our brain plays tricks on us. Have you heard of déjà vu? It's the feeling that something already happened, the feeling that you've been somewhere before even when you haven't. Some people say it's a psychic experience, a type of premonition or a throwback to a past life. But there is a neurobiological explanation. You don't actually remember, you just think you do. Your brain was badly damaged and that really affected your memory. So it's totally unsurprising that you'd get a false memory like this. Has anything else like this happened?"

I think of the woman in white. Should I tell him about her? He'll probably think I'm crazy. "No."

"Good. I know this is really hard on you, son. Bearing in mind the way things are, I think it's best you stop watching Eyestream for a while. Do you want to explore Middle-earth for a bit?"

"No, thanks," I say, glad that my computer voice hides my disappointment and frustration.

"Well, that's up to you. But please be careful. I have to insist you don't contact anyone else, not even anonymously. Do you promise?"

"Yes, okay."

"And I'll tell Pieter that too. Just ask him to take you anywhere you want to go—it's better than watching strangers. But he's not allowed to talk to anyone—at least, not on your behalf. You understand, right?"

"Please don't give him a hard time. He was just doing what I asked."

"I know, but he shouldn't have. How does it look for him to bribe some girl on your behalf? And in public too?"

"She wanted the money," I argue, even though I have to admit he's right: It didn't look good. LittleDevil sold her friend's identity to a stranger and Pieter used my name. Even though I never asked him to do it, I still feel bad about the whole thing.

"I'm really sorry, but I need to work for a bit. We can talk later. And don't take it all to heart. Don't read too much into it if strange things happen. Your brain was badly damaged and will sometimes play tricks on you. Let me know if anything else unusual happens, so I can let your doctors know."

"I understand, Dad. Thanks."

"Okay, then. See you later, son."

His picture disappears and the walls are white again. There's something calming about the stillness. Or it isn't unsettling, anyway.

What's actually going on here? One thing's for sure, there's either something wrong with me or the man claiming to be my father is lying. But why would he? What would be the point?

No matter how hard I try, I see no reason why he would lie to me. The idea seems a little paranoid. I'm only thinking all this because I don't remember my past, and can't be sure that the man I've been talking to actually is my father. I wish I could remember! All the uncertainty would fall away and that uneasy fear would just disappear. I'd still be nothing more than a mind without a body, a brain in a jar, but at least I'd know who I am—or who I was, anyway. There's nothing worse than not knowing.

But what can I do to get my memory back? I ask Alice to bring up my mother's pictures and the ones in the file with my name. I see a boy who must be me but is a total stranger: playing in the backyard, playing soccer, holding a certificate for winning a math competition, at the wedding of some woman I don't recognize, in church for his confirmation. The boy in the pictures has a past, that's for sure, but it doesn't feel like mine.

This won't get me anywhere. I need to find another way: If I can prove to myself that Julia is just a déjà vu experience, then at least I'll know my father is right.

I get Alice to open Nymochat and enter "July2001" in the search box. No hits. Strange. Has she changed her username? Or blocked me? I set up a new Nymochat account, just in case, but the search result is the same. There's no July2001.

Next, I open Eyestream and search for LittleDevil, but she doesn't come up either. Have they both closed their accounts? But why?

I feel scared, without really knowing why.

"Alice, open Pietercam."

A message tells me Pieter is offline. Something isn't right here. Something is really wrong. I feel like the ground is falling away and that I'm tumbling into a pit, like there's no solid ground under my feet, just a white, illuminated surface inside a virtual room.

CHAPTER 9

What do I know? What can I actually be sure of? How can I tell the difference between illusion and reality, memory and false memory?

I try to look at my situation rationally but don't have much to go on: I'm in a virtual room and don't have a physical body or a past, but allegedly have a damaged brain that gives me unreliable information. There's a man who claims to be my father. A girl who I think I know and who claims to be my sister—or at least, the sister of someone called Manuel who is a lot like me. The only way I can contact her is through either Nymochat or Eyestream, but both accounts have disappeared. The only thing I know for sure is that these two versions of reality are totally irreconcilable: Either Julia is my sister, in which case my father is lying to me for reasons I don't understand, or she isn't my sister, in which case my brain is lying. But how am I ever going to find out the truth when my own memory plays tricks on me? I can't even be sure that my chat with Julia actually happened. That I didn't just dream it.

Maybe it's all just a dream.

As far as I know I never believed in you, but God, if you do exist, please let me wake up and realize this is all just a nightmare. Please!

God isn't listening, and I don't blame him. But a picture suddenly appears on the wall—it's Pieter, standing in front of a mirror wearing camera glasses.

"You wanted to talk to me, boss?"

"Yes. This is going to sound really weird, but did you go to a shopping center with me today and pay a girl two hundred euros so she would give you the username of a person called Julia?"

He hesitates. "Why do you ask?"

"Did you or didn't you do it?"

"Yes, I did. Your father wasn't too pleased, I can tell you. You didn't have to tell him, you know. I'm just glad he didn't sack me on the spot."

"I'm sorry." My computer voice doesn't give away my relief. At least those memories are real. "Do you remember the username?"

"You don't?"

"I do, but may have misremembered."

"Hold on . . . it was Julia2001, I think. No, not Julia, July." I type the name into the Nymochat search box but, once again, her account doesn't come up. "Julia2001" doesn't show any results either.

"I spoke to Julia before, through the Nymochat account, but the connection shut down and now the account's gone."

"Hmm. You spoke? What about?"

"I asked her how she knew me. She said that, if what I said is true, she's my sister."

"I didn't think you had a sister."

"That's what I don't understand."

"Maybe she has a brother called Manuel. It's not exactly an uncommon name."

"That would be quite a coincidence, don't you think?"

"No idea. Maybe she wanted to trick you. Most likely the little crook who took my money is behind it all. It was a dumb thing to do. She probably got scared. Realized that what she's doing is actually fraud and quickly closed the account."

I'm not convinced. On the other hand, I haven't got a better theory.

"Don't take it so hard. Your memory will come back. Just be a little patient, kid."

Easy for him to say. "Yeah, I'll try. Thanks for everything."

"Just doing my job. You need anything else?"

"No, thanks. I'll be in touch if I do."

"Got it, boss."

I close the connection and open Eyestream. I can't find LittleDevil and Julia, but maybe I can trigger some more déjà vu. If I see another familiar face and can prove I've never met that person, then at least I'll know my father's right.

Once again, I click through the streams of mostly young people who unthinkingly share everything with the rest of the world. I can't decide whether Eyestreamers are generous or incredibly naive;

either way I'm grateful to watch life through their eyes. It's a poor substitute for having my own life but better than nothing, and when I look through their cameras, even if it's just for a bit, I forget the suffocating constraints of this room, my prison cell.

Faces glide past, tourist attractions drift across the wall. To save time, I activate six streams at once and get Alice to project them across the four walls of my white cube.

"That would make my head spin," a woman's voice says next to me.

I turn, startled. A woman's avatar stands at my side. She has shoulder-length brown hair and black-rimmed glasses, is wearing jeans, trainers, and a T-shirt with a black-and-white photograph of an old man and the words: *It is easier to go to Mars than it is to penetrate one's own being. C. G. Jung.*

"Who are you?"

"My name is Dr. Eva Hausmann. You can call me Eva. I'm a psychologist. Didn't your father mention me?"

"No. He did not."

"In that case, I'm sorry to just burst in here. Though I expect you're used to surprises by now."

"I'm not sure anyone ever gets used to surprises."

"No, of course not. I didn't mean anything by it. Do you want to tell me what you're doing here?"

"I'm looking for my past."

"By staring over random people's shoulders?"

"Sadly, I can't just go out and walk around for myself." My

computer voice masks my bitterness, but Eva seems to pick up on it anyway.

"Sorry. I was trying to understand, not judge you."

"I'm hoping to see someone else I recognize out there."

"So you'll get back more memories?"

"Either that, or be sure my memories are messed up."

"Your father said you were having déjà vu experiences. That's totally normal in your situation. Your brain is under extreme stress, not just because of your injuries but because of the implants too."

"The implants?"

"Did your father not tell you that his team implanted electrodes in your brain? How else would you be able to experience this virtual world and talk to me?"

"Well, yes, he just didn't give me the details."

She explains how a team of neurosurgeons have operated on me twenty-three times and that I'll need more surgery to increase and improve the interfaces between my brain and the computer. In fact, she says there's a lot of stuff that isn't working properly: I have no sense of touch, can't smell and taste things, and my computer voice could be better.

It's as though she's expecting me to be pleased about these future operations, but I'm doubtful. "Maybe I don't want to be improved."

Eva's avatar gives an artificial smile. "We're not out to improve *you*, just the way you interact with the world."

"What's the point? I already have a car, a drone, and a person at my beck and call. There's not much here to smell or touch."

"Not here maybe, but out there, in the world your father wants to create for you."

"You mean Middle-earth?"

"Exactly. Imagine what it would be like if you could walk around Elrond's palace and smell the flowers, or feel the wind in your hair as you fly on the back of an eagle . . ."

"Did he send you here to talk me into going back?"

"What makes you say that?"

"I think he was pretty disappointed that I didn't want to stay. He doesn't want to force me—though he could probably just shut down this white room and keep me in Middle-earth."

"Yes, he could. But, as you say, that way you'd be like a prisoner. And that's the last thing he wants. He loves you, Manuel. He's invested a huge chunk of his wealth so you can have a halfway bearable life. I don't think that much money has ever been put into saving one person."

"Maybe he should just have had me wake up in Middle-earth. That way I'd never have known I was ever anything other than a hobbit or an elf or a dwarf."

"We discussed that option. But it would have been wrong. You would always have felt something wasn't right. We wanted to give you the chance to find out the truth and decide for yourself whether you wanted to go into the fantasy world and stay there. That's the only way you'd be happy there."

"We? You mean this was your idea? The white room and me finding out who I am for myself?"

"The decision emerged from a discussion between me, your father, and some of the technical team. I certainly played a role but they were mostly his ideas."

"So why did he send you?"

"He didn't send me. He allowed me to talk to you."

"And why do you want to talk to me?"

"To make you face the truth."

My computer voice gives out a humorless laugh, which is exactly how I want it to sound. "The truth? Which truth? That none of this is real? That my body's nothing more than a useless slab of meat, supplying my brain with food and oxygen? That I'll never be able to run, play soccer, or eat an apple?"

"The truth is, you'll never get your memory back, Manuel. It has been irreparably damaged."

I stare at the wall, unable to take in any of the Eyestream images playing in front of me.

It takes me a while to find the words: "So . . . so my father lied to me when he said I'd be getting my memory back soon? He knew the whole time it would never happen?"

"Yes, he knew. He lied because he cares, Manuel. Because he loves you, you could say. He couldn't bring himself to tell you everything straightaway. I advised him to tell you everything from the start, but he disagreed. He was worried you'd lose the will to live. But now that he sees how desperately you're trying to recover your memory, he's realized he was wrong."

I want to close my eyes and shut out the camera images coming at me from all sides. But I can't even do that. There's no point to anything. I want to cry but can't make tears, and my computer voice can't even muster up a sob.

All I can do is say in a monotone: "And what am I supposed to do now?"

"Come with me to Middle-earth. You'll see, you'll like it. You may not have any memories of your former life but you're young enough to start a new one. It'll be a life lived in a fantasy world. You can be a hero, a sorcerer, a ruler. You'll fight evil and win. You're the first ever person to have this opportunity. Millions of young people across the world would envy the chance."

And I would swap places with any one of them. Except I can't. "I'll think about it."

"Good," Eva replies. "Let your father or me know once you've decided."

Her avatar disappears. I stare at the pictures around me, unsuccessfully trying to get used to the idea that I'll never really know who I was before the disaster that catapulted me out of reality and into this dream world. In the end, I ask Alice to shut down the pictures and dim the virtual room walls until I'm in total darkness.

I have no body. No memories. And now all my senses have been switched off. I'm nothing more than a mind lost in space.

I wish I could switch my mind off too. That I could just stop existing.

CHAPTER 10

The walls brighten even though I haven't asked Alice to do this.

"Good morning, Manuel."

"Have I been . . . asleep?"

"I don't understand the question."

"What time is it?"

"It is eight thirteen a.m."

I feel strangely heavy. As though my virtual body somehow has more substance. I touch my left arm with my right hand and I'm stunned: I can feel! It's like I'm wearing thick gloves, but when I run my fingers over my virtual clothes, I feel definite pressure.

"What happened?" I shout, unnerved by this sudden improvement. Alice doesn't understand the question.

"Alice, contact my father."

A short while later his avatar appears in my white room.

"Hello, son. I see you've come around."

"Come around? What do you mean?"

"You had surgery. We discussed it yesterday."

I stare at him. "We spoke about it?"

"Don't you remember?" he says. His simulated face is blank, but he sounds concerned.

"All I remember is talking to Eva, the psychologist. Then I asked Alice to turn the lights off. I wanted to think quietly for a bit. That feels like a few seconds ago."

"You spoke to Dr. Hausmann over two days ago, Manuel. She told me you'd spoken. I came, and you said you were ready to go back to Middle-earth. I was really pleased, of course, and suggested we bring forward an operation that would increase the interface between your brain and the computer. You agreed. The operation took longer than planned but was successful. Even though you don't remember anything that happened since right before the surgery."

I stare at him, speechless. It's too much to take in. How can I lose two days like that?

"Alice, open Eyestream!"

The site appears on one of the walls. The location, date, and local time for all livestreams from across the world show on the home page. My last visit really was two days ago.

"I'm sorry this is even more confusing. But I think losing two days' worth of memories is a small price to pay for everything you've gained. Anyway, you were under anesthetic most of that time." He opens his arms wide.

I step toward him, tentatively. His arms envelop me, and it feels really good. He sobs quietly.

It dawns on me that I have to stop fighting the truth and accept my fate, even though all the strange feelings, mixed-up memories, and contradictory statements don't make sense. I'll go crazy if I keep questioning everything. Maybe one day I'll find a logical explanation for it all, and know why I seem to recognize Julia, and why she claims to be my sister even though it's impossible. But until then, I have to live with the fact that I don't know—and that I may never know. I have to accept my father's massive gift, even though it isn't what I would have chosen.

After a while, my father lets go. "How about a short walk around Rivendell?"

"Not yet," I say. "I'd like to talk to Pieter first." I trust Pieter, I realize, more than I trust my own father.

"To Pieter?" He sounds disappointed. "Well, sure, if you like. I'll tell him to come."

My father vanishes and Pieter's avatar appears soon after.

"Hi, boss. How are you doing?"

"Really well, I think. Could you do me a favor? Could you punch my arm?"

"What?"

"Please, just do it."

"All right." He steps closer and gently punches my left arm.

"Harder!"

He hits me again, harder. Now *that* I feel. It's probably the happiest I've ever felt about experiencing pain.

"Ow!"

"That hurt?"

"Yes, it did." I can't help grinning.

"Sorry, but you asked me to."

"No need to apologize. I'm happy I can feel pain. Really happy!"

"Yes, that is good. I heard you had more surgery. It seems to have done the job."

"Looks that way. But that's not the only reason I wanted you to come. I wanted to ask you something. I spoke to the psychologist person and my father. They suggest I go and live in Middle-earth."

"You mean Middle-earth with all the dwarves and dragons and sorcerers?"

"Yes. My father had it built for me. I didn't want to go at first, but now . . . I think I'm ready to try again. Just not on my own. I wanted to ask if you would come with me."

"Come with you? How do you mean?"

"I'd like you to spend as much time with me in the virtual world as possible. As though you were playing a computer game all day long."

"Hmm. I've never really been into computer games. But sure, if that's what you want."

"Thanks, Pieter."

I contact my father and tell him I'm ready to go to Middle-earth. He's really pleased. Soon the walls of my room evaporate and I'm standing in front of Elrond's palace in Rivendell along with my father in his elf costume, a young elven woman carrying a bow, and a dwarf with a giant battle-ax.

"Why are you all so big?" the dwarf says in Pieter's voice.

I can't help laughing.

"Great that you decided to come back," my father says. He sweeps his hand to take in the whole valley. "All this is yours. You just need to decide which role you want to play. You could be the ruler of the elf kingdom if you like, or a powerful sorcerer."

"No, thanks. I'd like to be a regular elf, like Legolas." I think he was my favorite character in the book.

"Lego who?" Pieter wants to know.

"Have you never read *The Lord of the Rings*?"

"No. There's no time for that stuff when you're fighting insurgents in the Congo."

"In that case, it's entirely appropriate that you should play a hot-headed dwarf in this world," the other elf says in Eva's voice.

"Let's stay in character, please," my father urges. "From now on no one gets to talk about the Congo or anything else from out there in the real world. We're in Middle-earth now, in the year 2793 of the Third Age. Bilbo Baggins, who is destined to find the One Ring, is not yet born. Evil Sauron is building his strength in Mordor, but isn't yet powerful enough to engage in open warfare with other peoples. He relies on intrigue, bribery, abduction, murder, and other evil means to expand his reach, while Gandalf the Grey opposes him wherever he can. We are living in a time of great uncertainty, shifting alliances, and conflict. Humans have all but forgotten the threat from the East, and fight one another. The elves do their best to remain neutral but keep being drawn into battle. Recently, there has been an increase in orc attacks on human villages. The Riders of Rohan, who are unable to fully protect their sprawling kingdom, have turned to dwarves and elves for help. Pieter, you have come to Rivendell to talk us into granting the Rohirrim's request."

"You what?" the dwarf grumbles.

"A gentler tone is fitting, Sire Dwarf, if you are to seek our help," Eva says.

"Never before have dwarves needed the help of elves!" Pieter bellows. "We simply wish to grant you an opportunity to reap the rewards of our celebrated acts of heroism."

"You're really getting into character!" my father says, clearly pleased. "Right, son, are you ready to fight evil alongside your companions, Eva and Dwarf Pieter?"

"Shouldn't we change our names?" I say. "Eva doesn't sound very elfin."

"What about Evandiel?" the elf asks.

"Well, I'll keep Pieter, if that's all right with you," the dwarf says. "It's hard enough getting my bearings in this strange world without having to remember a new name. The worst bit is that I keep having to look up at you!"

The elf laughs gently. "So, let's just keep our own names. Agreed, Manuel?"

"Yes, okay."

"So, are you in?" the dwarf wants to know.

I feel the wind whip through my long elfin hair. "Of course I'm in!"

"Great," my father says. "If you agree, for now I'll be the Elf Prince. I have a mission for you . . ."

CHAPTER 11

The village lies in an idyllic spot next to a wide river. It looks peaceful in the evening sun, but according to the Elf Prince's account, orcs conquered the village a long time ago and it's now a base for terrible raids against humans.

I lift my hand and the dozen computer-controlled elf warriors, marching behind me like a robot army in perfectly synchronized lockstep, come to a stop. "Wait here!" I order.

"Yes, sire!" the squad leader replies.

Eva, Pieter, and I edge closer. Figures are visible in the distance, but they don't look like orc soldiers. They move around busily, but don't seem to be preparing for battle. One is feeding a dozen pigs wallowing in a sty; two others are using large pitchforks to stack hay. An orc—a female, maybe?—is even taking dry laundry off a washing line. There are no visible barricades or security measures.

"Is this supposed to be a base camp?" Pieter voices my confusion.

"Appearances can be deceptive," Eva says. "We should attack while we still have the element of surprise."

"It looks like the orcs have turned into peaceful village folk," I argue. "See the one over there on the left, feeding the pigs?"

"Orc farmers? Have you ever read Tolkien?"

"I don't know, have I?" I say, with a hint of sarcasm.

"Sorry. I just mean that orcs need to eat too, so it's hardly surprising they'd keep pigs for food. But that doesn't make them peace-loving farm folk."

At that moment a stout orc—this one is definitely female—emerges from a house. Two tiny creatures run along behind her.

"Since when do orcs have kids?" I say, stunned. "I thought they were manufactured in some kind of factory, like robots."

"That's really unusual," Eva agrees. "I've never heard of orc children. But maybe this world's rules aren't exactly the same as Tolkien's rules. Or maybe they're not little orcs but some other kind of creature."

"So now what?" Pieter asks. "Should we attack, or do you want to wait for nightfall?"

"I want to take a closer look," I reply.

"I'm coming with you!" the psychologist insists.

"No," I say decisively. "I'll go alone!" Pieter's so clumsy he would only hold me up, and whenever I'm with Eva I always feel like I'm being watched. Like she's a chaperone.

"He's the boss," Pieter says, before Eva can argue.

"All right. But be careful. I don't trust all this blissful tranquility."

"Don't worry. I'll be fine."

The closer I get, the stronger my impression that these orcs aren't at all hostile. Two guards are on duty, but their weapons are propped against the wall of an old barn while they sit on the grass bickering loudly over a game of dice. The perfect setup for a surprise attack. But I can't help thinking it's also the perfect setup for slaughtering helpless creatures. Which is absurd, I know: This is just a computer simulation and the orcs are just a series of computer models and graphic files. They have no feelings and no free will, but still . . .

I hide behind a hillock and monitor the village. A good dozen orcs, mostly unarmed, live here. I could finish them off on my own. Even if they were armed and ready for battle, they'd stand no chance against my experienced elf warriors.

That thought clinches my decision. It might cost the crucial element of surprise, but I first want to make sure that a fight can't be avoided. I leave my hiding place and head toward the village in plain view.

By the time the guards see me, I'm only twenty steps away. They stop their squabbling and stare at me. One screams in terror. They jump up and run into the village, leaving their weapons resting against the barn. Hearing the scream, the other orcs flee into their houses. By the time I get to the village there's no one in sight. I stand in the center of the settlement, outside a big building that might have been a tavern in days gone by.

"Hey, orcs!" I yell. "I want to talk to you! Is there anyone here who speaks my language?"

"What do you want?" an orc says from behind the closed door of the big building.

"I want you to leave this village immediately. We will allow you to leave in peace. If you fight back we will be forced to kill you."

"You be come alone?" the orc says. "Where is the army of yours?"

"My army is waiting for my order to attack!"

"You elf leader?"

"Yes, I am the leader."

"Good! Elves never let orcs to kill leader. You good hostage!"

With these words the door swings open and three heavily armed orcs leap out. Orc warriors spring from the other houses too. They were hiding. I fell into the trap like a fool!

I draw my sword. Maybe I can keep the orcs at bay until help arrives. With any luck, Pieter and Eva are watching and will already know I'm in trouble.

I'm surrounded by orcs. They turn their swords and spears on me but seem scared and don't dare engage in close combat. They must have had bad experiences with elf warriors in the past. But still, I'm so outnumbered I don't stand a chance.

I give a wild roar and run at the orc leader, push the ground away with all my strength, spring onto his shoulders, and jump from there onto the building wall. I grab the edge of the roof and pull myself up in one elegant swing. The whole maneuver takes milliseconds and wouldn't have been possible in a world governed by the laws of gravity. But we're in Middle-earth, I'm an elf, and my father has equipped my virtual body with a few unfair advantages.

The orcs seem as surprised as I am by the successful maneuver. They stare up and shout in confusion. I calmly nock an arrow onto my bow and they spring into action, running off in different directions. Two head toward a large barn and pull back a heavy bolt. I assume they're planning to hide, but then there's a terrible roar and suddenly a colossus with gigantic muscles and a disproportionally tiny head boulders out of the barn. A troll!

Oh boy! I feel pure panic and forget for a moment that none of this is real.

The troll looks around searchingly. He sees me and takes a running jump at the roof, but is too heavy to reach it. Instead, he slams his massive fists against the wall. The wood cracks, and the whole building shakes. I almost lose consciousness.

I aim an arrow at his eye, but the monster keeps bludgeoning the building and I can't hold the bow still.

"Hold on, kid!" Pieter yells. He runs forward, flailing an ax just as an arrow flies from Eva's bow over his head. It pierces the troll's ear and lodges in his muscular neck, but it's just a mosquito bite to the monster. He tears a hole in the wall like it's made of cardboard. The whole structure sways uncontrollably, then there's a terrible crash and the roof gives way under me. I try to hold on but the building collapses. Tiles and wooden beams fall around me—but that's nothing compared to the moment the troll rips away the wall and throws himself at me. I don't even have time to hold up my sword for protection. His enormous paws grab me and lift me up, spinning me around like a club. My head slams into the wreckage and the world turns black.

CHAPTER 12

"You caused a real mess falling for that one," Pieter says. He's standing at my bedside next to my father, Eva, and Alandil. We're inside Elrond's palace in a chamber decorated with elaborate murals. It feels as though only seconds have gone by since the troll got me. Maybe it really is just that long.

My body is covered in bruises. I'm in pain—and could scream with happiness! The virtual world is getting more realistic. Maybe my life isn't over.

"Shouldn't I be dead?" I ask.

"Elves don't die that easily," my father says.

"We took care of the troll before he could rip you to shreds," Eva explains. "But it was close."

"Alandil will take care of you until you're better," my father says.

The elf gives a small bow. "I hope the pear grass juice is helping with the pain, sire."

"Please take more care next time," my father scolds. "Elves are tough—not immortal."

"What happens if I do actually die? Here in the virtual world, I mean? Do I just spawn to the palace?"

"What the heck is 'spawning'?" Pieter asks.

"It's when you die in a computer game and the character reappears in a preprogrammed place, and you have to play from there."

"Like being reborn? Wouldn't it be great if that could happen in real life?"

"Best you don't let things get that far," my father says. "We'll leave you to rest now. Feel better."

"Thanks."

They leave the room, but Alandil stays behind. "Anything else, sire?"

"Could you please stop calling me 'sire,' Alandil? My name is Manuel."

"As you wish, Manuel."

I chat with the elf for a while. She pauses every now and then when there's something she hasn't understood, but most of her responses are surprisingly on point. After a while I almost forget she's just a simulated character. My father and his team must have put in a massive amount of work to make her so intelligent. He's gone to a lot of trouble to give me the chance of a decent life.

Eventually, Alandil leaves. She says she has other patients to attend. When I'm alone, I realize how much I enjoy her company.

Is it possible to become friends with a computer simulation? I get up and pace the room restlessly. My body hurts with every move, but I'm glad of the pain. In the end, I pull open the folding doors and step onto the balcony. A chill wind blows off the mountains and I feel cold. I hold on to the feeling like I'm greeting a long-lost friend. Did I feel this much when I first arrived, or have the doctors improved my brain's interface even more?

My gaze rests on the row of balconies to my left. There's a woman with long black hair on a balcony two rooms away. She's wearing a simple white dress. I stare; she turns slowly, then smiles.

I race out of the room, practically running into Pieter, Eva, and my father.

"What's going on?" the dwarf says, but I push past him and pull open the second door along the corridor.

It's empty, and so is the balcony. Did I get the wrong room? I go outside, but there's no woman in white on any of the balconies.

I head back to my room feeling seriously uneasy.

"What's the matter?" Eva wants to know.

"The woman in white. She was here. Outside on one of the balconies."

"What woman in white?"

"I saw her at the cemetery, when I went to visit my mother's grave with Dad. And then again on Eyestream. And now here."

"And you think it's the same person?"

"How's that even possible?" asks Pieter.

"I have no idea," I admit. "But she looked exactly the same as the first two times I saw her. It feels like I know her from before."

"Manuel, we already talked about déjà vu," Eva says.

"How can it be déjà vu when I see the same person in different places?"

"Maybe it's not exactly that. It sounds more like a hallucination. You see someone who triggers something, pain or a deep emotion perhaps. Your brain alters that person's face so it looks like a person from your subconscious. That's why you think it's always the same person. It was probably just a simulation of an elf woman."

"So what did she look like, this woman in white?" my father says. I describe her as best as I can.

"That's your mother, kid," he replies.

"No. I may not remember my mother, but I've seen enough pictures of her. She looks a lot like her but it isn't her."

"Maybe the hallucination was triggered by a trauma?" Pieter suggests.

The expression on Eva's avatar is neutral, but she sounds dismissive. "So *you're* the psychologist now?"

"Just saying," the dwarf answers, lifting his hands in surrender.

My father agrees with Pieter: "I don't think it's such a bad idea. A woman in white could be a doctor or a nurse. Maybe Manuel saw someone when he was close to death, and that image was the last one that imprinted on his damaged brain."

"I agree it can't be ruled out," admits Eva. "The fact that it looks like his mother could explain why he clings to the picture. Even so, it is a sensory delusion. You might have more, Manuel. But I hope they'll become less frequent over time."

Her explanation isn't convincing. If I'm having hallucinations, why just that one? Or am I seeing other stuff that isn't real?

I suddenly realize how ridiculous the question is and a bitter laugh escapes from my mouth. In my computer voice it sounds like a dog barking. Nothing I'm looking at in this world is real. What difference does it make whether or not I imagine a woman in white?

Alandil arrives. She's carrying a patterned board with silver and ivory figures. "I see you're feeling better, sire . . . I mean, Manuel." The way she corrects herself halfway through the sentence makes her seem incredibly human, even though her voice is unmistakably simulated. "I thought you might be bored and enjoy a game. But I see you have company."

"We were just leaving," my father says, nodding at Pieter and Eva. They follow him out of the room without saying a word.

"Sorry. I don't know this game," I say as she sets the board on the table.

"That's all right, Manuel. I'll explain the rules." We sit. The game is vaguely like chess, except the board has six sides, there are fewer pieces and they move around differently.

Alandil is a good and patient teacher, so it doesn't take me long to understand the basics. Even though there are few rules, it's incredibly complicated. Obviously, I'm fully aware there's no way I can win against a computer program. Even so, by the third round, the game goes to me.

"I concede defeat," the elf says. "You're a fast learner, Manuel."

"You let me win," I say.

She smiles. "You got me! Another game?"

"Definitely."

This time she shows her real skill and decimates my army in ten moves.

"That was impressive," I say.

"Sorry. I couldn't help myself. I find it hard to hold back. But it's not really fair. I've been playing this game for over a thousand years and you just learned two hours ago."

"You're a machine. No wonder you're so good at the game." I regret my words as soon as I've said them. Maybe I'm being mean because my pride has been hurt.

She stares at me for a second. "I'm a machine? What do you mean?"

Now I'm the one who's speechless. Did she really understand what I said? Is her intelligence so highly developed that she's capable of self-reflection? No, of course not. It's just that some programmer was smart enough to predict I'd say something like that, and coded a suitable response.

Pieter walks in before I can test the programmer's skills some more.

Alandil gets up. "I should leave you alone."

I'm a little sad she's going.

"She's pretty!" Pieter says.

Lucky that my avatar can't blush and only has a synthetic voice so he can't hear my embarrassment. "Ah . . . so do you feel like playing a game of Dwarves and Giants?"

"Are you trying to offend me?"

"No, it's a game. Alandil just taught me. Of course, she's awesome at it, but that's no surprise. Computers are way better at this type of game than humans."

"Don't you think you should stop seeing the world like a simulation? It might be easier for you to stay if you thought of it as real."

I don't like what he's saying. "Don't you think I've forgotten enough already?"

"Sorry, Manuel. I didn't mean it like that. And you're right, you shouldn't forget anything. But it wouldn't hurt to let yourself get a little more carried away in the illusion. I mean, if you like the elf girl . . ."

"What do you mean?"

"Nothing. Never mind. Actually, I only came to ask how you're doing, and when you think you'll be ready to get back out there."

"I don't know. But bearing in mind the troll must have pounded all my bones, Alandil's potion is pretty powerful. Maybe by tomorrow I'll feel like nothing happened."

"Good. We could use your help. We managed to get the orcs out of the village, but they've joined ranks with other orcs nearby and are planning a revenge attack on Edoras, the capital of Rohan. We have to warn the Rohirrim and help defend the town."

"Are you sure I'll be any use?"

"It should be fine so long you as you don't try to sit down with the orcs over a cup of raspberry tea and try to get them to join the

United Nations. You shouldn't really be at the front line, but you're smart, so you can help us plan our strategy."

"No problem, I've learned my lesson. Can it wait until tomorrow?"

"I guess. Rest up and give Alandil a chance to do her job."

Instead of leaving by the door, Pieter just disappears into thin air. He must have logged out of the simulation and is probably heading out to some bar. Lucky man.

The setting sun lights the sky an almost tacky pink. I go onto the balcony to watch the spectacle, which looks completely natural and otherworldly at the same time, as though it had been painted by Caspar David Friedrich. *How the heck do I know who Caspar David Friedrich is?*

"It's time for your dressings, Manuel."

Alandil has appeared in my room soundlessly. Maybe she teleported here. Who knows what happens in this simulation when no one's watching.

"For my what?"

"I need to change your dressings. Please remove your clothing."

I'm reluctant to strip in front of her. It takes a few seconds before I remember she's just a computer simulation and that my body isn't real. I pull off the delicate fabric of my floor-length tunic, and I'm surprised to find that my virtual body is almost completely covered in bandages, like I'm an Egyptian mummy.

"Here, drink this!" Alandil holds out a beaker filled with an oily liquid. "It doesn't taste good but will help with the pain."

I don't bother explaining that I can't taste anything, or that I welcome the pain because it means I sort of still have a body. I swallow the liquid without speaking. I really can't taste anything but feel warmth spread through me. I'm a little woozy.

"Please lie down."

I follow her instructions and watch her skillfully and carefully change my dressing. Every hand movement seems completely real. Sometimes I even wince in pain when she removes a dressing from a sensitive area. She looks at me with concern every time and apologizes for her ineptitude.

It doesn't matter how hard I try, Alandil seems less and less like a straightforward NPC—a computer-simulated character without emotion, senses, or intelligence. Everything about her makes her seem like an actual person. And a really nice one at that.

"Thank you," I say when she's finished covering my wounds in a soothing green herbal paste. "I feel less like I've just been through a meat grinder."

"That pleases me, Manuel." She gives a brief smile, but is frowning. She looks worried. "Soon you will return to battle?"

Something bugs me about her reply, but I'm not sure what. "Isn't that why I'm here?" I ask.

"I cannot say. But I . . . I wouldn't like anything to happen to you."

I have a bad thought. "Don't worry, I was always really good at *World of Warcraft*," I say casually.

"This isn't a game, Manuel. If another troll gets you, I don't know whether my healing arts will be enough to keep you alive."

I knew it! "How do you know about *World of Warcraft*? And how do you even know what it might feel like to go through a meat grinder?"

"What? No, you misunderstood. I'm just a simple serving girl and know nothing of such things."

"Kiss me, Alandil!"

Her eyes widen, as though startled by the request. But then she leans forward, places her arm around my neck, closes her eyes, and presses her lips against mine. I feel the softness of her lips and her warm breath.

"I love you, Manuel," she whispers as her lips move away from mine.

The lie hits me like a stab in the back. What a naive idiot I've been! I push her away with all my strength and she falls back, stumbles, and lands on the floor.

She stares at me wide-eyed. "But, Manuel . . . what does this mean? Don't you want it?"

"Don't I want what?" My computer-generated voice hides my anger.

"That we . . . you and me . . . we could be happy!"

"You think? I doubt it. Who are you really?"

"I don't know what you . . . what you mean, sire."

"Oh yeah? I think you know just what I mean. For a while I really thought you were a pretty sophisticated piece of software.

But now I realize what's going on. Is that you, Eva? Was it your idea for me to fall in love with an empty shell?"

Eva walks into the room. "Manuel! Alandil! What's going on? I heard a noise—"

"Oh, what a coincidence!" I say as disparagingly as I can, even though my voice sounds just as flat as usual.

"Manuel, it's not what you think," Alandil tries to explain, but her voice sounds different now. It's not the artificial elf voice, but it's not Eva's either. A woman's voice, but not one I know.

"So what is it, then? Who are you?"

"My name is Katrin," she replies sheepishly. "I'm one of the designers that developed Middle-earth. Your father asked me to play the role of Alandil. He wanted you to have a friend in this world—a real friend who would really understand you. He didn't ask me to make you fall in love with me . . . but when you asked me to kiss you, I thought . . . I'm . . . I'm really sorry if I hurt you!"

"Tell it to the fairies, or whatever the Tolkien version of fairies is! Eva, I want to go back to the white room. Now!"

CHAPTER 13

'm back in my virtual prison. The walls are blank; there's nothing to hear, no breeze. I got my way. But at what price?

They spent at least half an hour trying to talk me around: my father, Eva, Pieter, and Katrin. They made me promises, asked for my forgiveness. They were desperate for me to stay in Middle-earth. But that just strengthened my resolve.

Except now that I'm back, the room feels horribly cramped, as though the luminous walls are closing in on me, crushing me. I really want to fill them with camera images just to get rid of the emptiness. But I fight the urge. I need to keep a clear head.

Cogito, ergo sum—I think, therefore I am. That's what the French philosopher René Descartes said. For some reason—maybe I wrote a paper on the subject in school—I know this Latin phrase comes from his book *First Meditations on Philosophy*. I even know by heart the passage where he explains his conclusion:

But there is a deceiver of supreme power and cunning who is deliberately and constantly deceiving me. In that case, I too undoubtedly exist, if he is deceiving me; and let him deceive me as much as he can, he will never bring it about that I am nothing so long as I think that I am something.

Descartes would have liked the white room. Here, it's really obvious how our senses deceive us: nothing I see, hear, or feel is real. None of my sense impressions can be trusted. I tried to forget that for a while. But Alandil's lie made me wake up and smell the coffee. What an idiot! Falling for the orcs' ploy wasn't nearly as dumb as believing that this supposedly superintelligent artificial intelligence wasn't actually a real person.

They probably meant well. But what's the point of living in a world where everyone means well? Where I can't even trust the fact that a computer simulation *is* a computer simulation? In a world like that, I'd be nothing more than a newborn, lying helplessly in its crib with no hope of ever growing up to be independent. What would be the meaning, the point, of my life? I'm floored by a feeling of deep despair. I just want to end this helpless, undignified existence—here, now. But I can't even do that.

Pieter's avatar appears. "Hello, Manuel. How are you doing?"

"Leave me alone."

"Shall I put on the camera glasses and get you out for a walk? It's a nice day!"

"No, thanks. I want to be left alone."

"If that's how you feel," he says resignedly, then disappears.

I don't trust him anymore. Which is probably unfair because Pieter isn't in a position to help. The thing with Alandil was almost definitely Eva's idea, or maybe my father's, but no way was it Pieter's. Still, he knew about it, that much I do know, and he didn't say anything. He may not have masterminded the lie, but he was complicit. Pieter probably meant well too. But I still can't forgive him.

Pieter's suggestion has given me an idea, though.

"Alice, what time is it?" I say, wondering whether Alice is a real person too, someone who is just acting really dumb.

"It is 8:15 p.m."

"Open Eyestream."

There's still no trace of LittleDevil, but there are lots of active streamers out and about in Hamburg. What Pieter said is true: It's a lovely evening. A weather website reports a temperature of almost 68°F. Perfect barbecue weather. There are no Eyestreamers in City Park, but luckily I don't need to rely on luck.

"Alice, take over ME-1."

The car's control panel appears on one of the walls. It's parked in the garage. I start the engine. The garage door opens automatically.

Twenty minutes later I stop at the edge of City Park and power up the drone, fly it up to a height of thirty yards, hover over a wide road, and head into the park, which is glimmering in the light of the setting sun. It feels strange to glide over the treetops like a bird . . . or a ghost.

A dozen small groups have gathered on a wide lawn and sit around disposable barbecue sets. I steer the drone so that I can systematically check everyone through the camera. Some people look up, part curious, part annoyed. A young man with a beard gives me the finger.

I start looking for Julia without really expecting to find her, circling over the park like a bird of prey, scanning the faces that tilt up toward me. A few more minutes pass by . . . and then, impossibly, I spot her. A sort of electric shock zaps through me when I see her face looking up, inquisitive. She's sitting on a blanket next to a man wearing a baseball cap that obscures his face.

She waves. Does she know it's me? No, of course not. She's just less hostile toward the mystery drone pilot than that guy who flicked me off. I've found her! But now what? I have no way to communicate with her. I lower the drone until it's hovering right in front of her.

"Manuel, is that you?" she shouts.

I move the drone up and down a few times, like a nod.

"Oh, God, Manuel!" She starts to cry.

The man next to her reaches out to grab the drone. Before I have time to move out of the way, he's got ahold of it and turned it around so he's looking straight into the camera. He has a gray-flecked beard, is wearing thick-rimmed glasses and a T-shirt with the picture of a white rabbit holding a pocket watch. *Follow me into the rabbit hole*, it says—a line from *Alice's Adventures in Wonderland*. I wonder how I know the book. Did my mother read it to me when I was a kid? Did I read it on my own?

"There's not much time, Manuel," the man says. "My name is

Marten Raffay. I used to be the business partner of the man holding you captive: Henning Jaspers. Whatever he's told you, don't believe him! He's just using you. Listen: You need to say this code so we can speak without being overheard . . ."

The wall showing the view from the drone's camera goes blank. An error message says the connection has failed.

"Alice, activate ME-4!"

"I can't connect to ME-4."

"Take over ME-1."

"I can't connect to ME-1."

My father's face appears on the wall. He doesn't look happy.

"Manuel! I thought we agreed you wouldn't try to contact anyone."

"Who is Marten Raffay?"

He sighs theatrically. "He was my business partner. We set up Dark Star together. He was the lead programmer. A brilliant mind. But the pressure got too much and he started taking drugs. He became paranoid, said I was betraying him, turning the team against him. I tried to support and help him for as long as I could, but it got too much for the whole team. In the end, we had to cut him off, to protect the company from further losses. As you can imagine, he wasn't happy about it. I've often wondered whether . . . I'm getting ahead of myself, there's no real evidence."

"Evidence of what?"

"That he's behind the attack on your mother, that he shot you. He had the technical knowledge to breach our security system, and

I wouldn't put it past him. At least, I wouldn't put it past the person he became. We used to be best friends, but he's not the same person now."

I push down the anger I've been feeling, determined to think clearly. "Didn't the police look into him?"

"Yes, of course. Like I said, we didn't find anything concrete against him. But he's still brilliant, even though he's insane. He may have outsmarted the investigators."

"What's his connection to Julia?"

"I don't know. It looks as though he's using her to contact you. I have no idea how he knows you were looking for her, but none of that matters. He wants to use you to get into our program. The fact he was trying to give you a code proves that."

"Were you watching the whole time?"

"Not me; Eva. It's her job to help you find your feet and lead a halfway decent life. To do that, she needs to know how you're feeling and what you're doing. Unfortunately, she didn't recognize Marten straightaway."

"So I'm being watched 24/7?"

"What did you expect? You're in a secured room with the most complex technology that's ever been used to keep a person alive. A team of doctors is continually working to make sure all the interfaces between your brain and the virtual system are operational, and that you're not developing an inflammation or a rejection reaction. Of course you're always being monitored. It's the only way to keep you alive."

"I mean here, in the virtual world."

"It's all part of the same thing. We can tell by what you do whether you're okay. I thought you understood that."

I have to admit it's pretty obvious. Did I really think this was some sort of private zone? I just didn't spend too much time thinking about it. Now I feel like I've been duped, that I've been a fool.

"What's this code thing all about?"

"Marten developed the simulation system's basic structure. When his paranoia increased, he built a sort of back door into the program so he could switch off the autonomous security system. It's the system that stops outsiders getting access and immediately triggers an alarm when something unusual happens. Someone inside the virtual world has to say a specific set of words to activate his code. If he'd managed to get someone to help him, he would have had full access to our server and been able to cause major damage."

"Who was going to help him?"

"He thought one of his former colleagues would help and tried to recruit various different people, but everyone knew he had issues. That's probably why he decided to use you. You don't remember him and don't know anything about his past, so all he had to do was convince you that I'm the enemy and that *he's* the only one that can help you."

"How do you know all this?"

"Marten was brilliant, but not the only bright spark at Dark Star. Our head of security found the malware and removed it a long time ago. Even if he had given you the code and you'd said it, nothing would have happened. By the way, it's '*Follow me into the rabbit hole.*'"

"That was on the front of his T-shirt."

"Exactly. He must have hoped you'd work it out for yourself and say the code words, even if he didn't have time to tell you."

"Is that why you shut the connection down?"

"No, if that was it then I wouldn't have just told you the code. Like I said, we found and removed his malware a long time ago."

"Why, then?"

"Do you think I'm just going to stand there and watch him fill your mind with his paranoid delusions? God knows you have enough on your plate, son. I'll contact the police. They should take another look at him. Maybe they'll find some evidence that he's behind your mother's murder. Either way, you have to promise me you won't try to contact him again."

"How could I, anyway?" I ask, sure that my computer voice is able to convey my bitterness. "I'm being watched all the time, and as soon as he shows up on camera, you cut the connection."

"So has he hit his mark?" my father says, his voice heavy with exhaustion and profound sorrow. "Has he polluted your mind with his paranoia so you think I'm lying? Don't you trust me anymore, son?"

"How am I supposed to know what's real and what isn't, Dad?" I want to cry, but can't make tears. "How can I tell the difference between truth and lies, insanity and reason, when I don't have a memory and can't rely on my senses?"

He looks at me silently, deeply disappointed. Then he nods. "I think I know what you mean. Just rely on your mind, son. If you can't help it, then question everything I say. But don't do anything rash. Don't let the man who may have killed your mother, the man who may be responsible for where you are now, take advantage of you."

With that, he cuts the connection, leaving me in the white room, sad and confused.

CHAPTER 14

My father asked me not to do anything rash. That strikes me as being pretty cynical. What can I do that might be rash? Nothing at all.

Days go by while I search the internet, randomly following Eyestreamers and reading ebooks about people in a persistent vegetative state. But nothing helps me unpick the tangle of thoughts in my head or find a bit of peace. I no longer have access to the car and drone. My father says Marten Raffay damaged the drone and that the car is at risk of being hacked, which is why he's had to take it off the network for now. In actual fact, he just wants to stop me trying to contact Julia or Raffay. At least, that's how I see it. Or is that exactly the kind of paranoia that sent Marten Raffay over the edge? Then again, who wouldn't be paranoid in my shoes?

Eva, my father, Pieter, even Katrin are all doing their best to cheer me up. At some point they stop trying to convince me to go back to Middle-earth. But they try to keep me company and make my situation more bearable. The result is the exact opposite.

I can't stand their false pity. So I refuse to speak to them or even acknowledge their presence. Their avatars showing up in my luminous prison cell is no different than them just watching me from outside where I can't see them.

I try to distract myself with films, documentaries, box sets, books, music, even games—I can access everything ever created by the human imagination. But nothing holds my attention for more than a few minutes, and nothing relieves my state of anxiety. I mostly give up after a few minutes.

The longer this excruciating situation goes on, the more I toy with the idea of just accepting my fate and going back to Middle-earth. Except next time it would be for good. But that would feel like a defeat. Even though I'm still hoping they all mean well, I don't want to grant them this victory. Not yet.

A few days later, I project Eyestreams across all six walls of the white room and try to reach a trancelike state by staring at strangers and switching off my thoughts. It's an attempt to dissolve my own awareness and blend into the people with camera glasses so I can get away from my own sad reality. And it works, at least for a while.

Suddenly I come to with a jolt. I don't know how long I've been zoned out, but I'm wide awake now. I saw something. Some detail from one of the cameras caught my attention. But which camera?

I watch the streams closely. They're all showing views of Hamburg. Was that my choice, or did Eyestream just automatically recommend pictures based on what might interest me? I don't know.

One of the cameras shows a view of the Outer Alster Lake taken from a rowboat. The weather's beautiful and, as it's Sunday, the Alster steamboats wind their way past a colorful throng of yachts. Nothing about the picture strikes me as unusual.

The second stream is taken from the market outside city hall and comes with a commentary from a girl speaking Mandarin. Did I see something in the crowd? I look for familiar faces or a woman in a white dress—but there's nothing.

A steamer on a port tour. The camera bobs up and down as the boat full of tourists plugs its way through the swell left by a ship. The guide's commentary is almost incomprehensible. Nothing here catches my attention either.

Young men play amateur football on a full-sized field. They're around my age. Quite a big guy with blond hair dribbles toward the opponents' goal, beats a defender, and shoots, but the ball flies over the bar and whacks into a graffiti-covered wall.

That's when I see it: graffiti of a white rabbit with a pocket watch, just like the one on Raffay's T-shirt. It's wearing a gold chain around its neck with the letter *C* on it.

My mind races as I stare at the streams blindly. What if it's a message? Looked at coldly, that seems really unlikely. And yet, I can only see it like a message. Even though I'm worried my father is right and Marten Raffay probably just wants to use me, my heart is racing. If Raffay, or even Julia, sprayed the white rabbit on the wall on the off chance I'd see it, then there have to be more clues.

My father and the others can't find out something's going on or they'll shut down Eyestream. They see what I see, but can't know what I'm reading into it. I have to be careful.

I pull new, quickly alternating streams up across the six walls. On the outside, I stay impassive. But inside I'm no longer in a switched-off trance. I'm wired and flinch every time I see a graffiti-sprayed wall. At some point, I realize they're probably measuring those responses too, so try to stay calm.

Hours go by without me finding any more rabbits with pocket watches. Slowly, I lose my conviction that the graffiti is for me. Then something else sends a shiver through me: on the gate of a rusty old shed, there's a cat with a big grin. On one section of the cat's purple fur, dark stripes form the letter *O*. I was looking out for the wrong thing. It would be much too obvious for white rabbit graffiti to suddenly start appearing all over town. Raffay has to be a lot subtler to contact me. The rabbit was just a clue to let me know the code they're using—ciphers from *Alice's Adventures in Wonderland*. The Cheshire Cat is another character in the book. How does Raffay know I've read it? Maybe I told him, or maybe he gave it to me.

Now that I know what I'm looking for, it's easier to find the symbols hidden in graffiti. I come across a playing card, the Queen of Hearts, but there's a *G* in the corner of the card instead of a *Q*. Sometime later, I see a smooth black top hat on a soundproof barrier near a train track—the Mad Hatter's emblem. There's a white *R* sprayed on it.

COGR. Whatever that is, it doesn't fit the quote on Raffay's

T-shirt. Because *Follow me into the rabbit hole* doesn't have a *G* or a *C*.

I keep searching for characters from *Alice's Adventures in Wonderland* and wonder why, if Marten Raffay really is as smart as my father says, he would be so obvious as to print the code words on a T-shirt. And if the Alice quote isn't the actual code, maybe the malware found by my father's security guy was just a decoy—and Raffay planted a second, better concealed, code. Maybe the point of the T-shirt was to give me a clue about what to look for. *Follow me into the rabbit hole.* It sounds like an instruction. I definitely don't have all the information I need to solve the puzzle, but it's quite clear that someone has hidden a coded message in graffiti all over town. At last I have something to do, a purpose, a goal.

But it takes a whole lot of patience. I have to watch hours' worth of video streams before my hard work is rewarded and I find another symbol from Lewis Carroll's story. It's a blue caterpillar drawing on a hookah, puffing out clouds of smoke. One of the clouds forms the letter *T*.

"How's it going, Manuel?"

I turn around, caught off guard. Eva's avatar has appeared at my side. "Do you have to burst in like that?"

"Sorry. We're just wondering what you're doing."

"What I'm doing? Is that a joke?"

"Not at all."

"I'm standing here watching video streams. Of course, I could just go out for a little stroll, but don't feel like it right now."

"Save the sarcasm, Manuel. You have all the options in the world. There are a hundred thousand paraplegics, and they'd all love to swap places with you."

"And I'd swap places with them if it meant I could see, smell, and taste what's real."

"You could come back to Middle-earth."

"Please, don't start that again!"

"Okay, all right. But we're worried about you, Manuel."

"Isn't that nice. Don't worry, I'm fine."

"Your brain-wave patterns are throwing up a few anomalies."

An ice-cold shiver runs down my back—at least that's how it feels. Can they actually read my mind? "What kind of anomalies?"

"Over the last few days, you've been passively watching those videos. Almost as though you were in a trance. We measured mostly theta waves, which are typically found in hypnotic states or right before sleep. But for the last while you seem to be wide awake, as though you're really focused on something."

I improvise. "I'm bored, so I made up a game: When a new Eyestreamer logs in, I take the first thing I see—say that fire engine crossing the junction there—and try to find something like it in one of the other streams. A bit like 'I spy with my little eye' but in single-player mode."

"We have a huge selection of computer games if you want to play."

"I know. But this game happens in the real world so it's more fun."

"Manuel, I don't want to pressure you, but if you could give us another chance in the world your father built for you, then—"

"Thanks for not pressuring me, Eva. Maybe another time. I'm not ready. And I'd like you to leave me alone."

"As you wish." Her voice sounds mildly offended but she leaves wordlessly.

Damn! I have to be careful. They'll probably watch me really closely now. When I find a new symbol, my brain waves probably reflect my excitement. At some point they'll work out what's going on and then it'll all be over.

My thought process surprises me. Do I really believe that the only people in my life are my enemies? I don't particularly like Eva but she seems to mean well. At least, up to now she hasn't given me a reason to think anything different—not to mention my father or Pieter, who are really kind. On the other hand, they control my every move and have told me everything I think I know about my situation. If they were lying, how would I know? Is it possible that Marten Raffay is telling the truth? The only way to be sure is to crack the code. But what if I cause serious damage? If the man who claims to be my father really is my father, then crazy Raffay will have achieved exactly what he set out to do: He will have used me as a weapon against his former business partner. And if he really did kill my mother . . . but that's all pure conjecture. Until I find the code, I don't need to decide whose side I'm on.

So I keep looking. Before long I find another symbol: a turtle with a calf's head, the Mock Turtle. There's a big *U* on his shell. I do my best to stay calm and stare at a stream from Reeperbahn while I string together the letters I've got so far: COGRTU. They don't make up a word. On the other hand, they're not in the right order, because Raffay couldn't have known which stream they'd show up in or when. So I try rearranging the letters: GORTUC, TROCGU, URGOCT. No, nothing.

Stream after stream flickers across the walls of the room that makes up my entire universe. After a while I start to play the game I told Eva that I'd made up. It's actually fun.

Just as I'm trying to find a woman wearing red shoes in one of the streams, I spot a train going past. It has graffiti of a weird bird that's like a cross between a comically plump eagle and a swan. It must be a dodo, another character from Lewis Carroll's story. The bird has a worm in its beak. It's twisted into a G shape.

CRGOTUG. That doesn't really help. But something occurs to me. The dodo appears in the story quite early on, when Alice falls into a lake of her own tears. What if Raffay put the letters in order of when the characters show up in the book?

I try it out. White Rabbit is first, so C goes at the beginning. Dodo comes soon after, then the Caterpillar, the Cheshire Cat, the Mad Hatter, the Queen of Hearts, and Mock Turtle right toward the end of the book. That makes CGTORGU. It's not much, but there must still be loads of symbols I haven't found yet—Bill the Lizard is still missing, the March Hare, and the Dormouse, which is the first creature Alice meets in Wonderland. That means there could be other missing letters that fit in between the ones I've already found: $C \ldots G \ldots T \ldots O \ldots R \ldots G \ldots U \ldots$

I randomly try out different vowels and consonants and suddenly a sentence jumps out at me. It perfectly matches the letters—and my situation.

I've found the answer.

CHAPTER 15

COGITO, ERGO SUM. I think, therefore I am: Marten Raffay's message. It's as though he totally understood my problem. There's only one thing I know for sure—I exist. My senses might fool me; only the fact of my existence is certain.

But am I being fooled? Just because it's possible doesn't mean it's true. René Descartes chose to question everything, and imagined an all-powerful demon that created an illusory world. But he didn't actually believe the world was an illusion—it was just a thought experiment to him. But to me, it's a bitter reality: All I see are projections on the walls of a white room. I can't even be certain that the Eyestreams playing on the walls are actually coming from real people and show a world that actually exists. Only my mind is real. But how can my mind help me find out what to do?

Assuming they even work, by saying the code words I'm choosing to activate Marten Raffay's hidden program. The man who's supposed to be my father will know I've betrayed him. Either way, I can't predict the consequences, and wouldn't be able to take things back. How can I make such a massive decision when there are so many unknowns?

Doing nothing seems just as impossible. If Raffay had contacted me on his own, I wouldn't take the risk—but Julia was with him and I can trust her, I feel it. But then, that feeling could be another illusion. And even if I can trust her, how do I know Marten Raffay isn't using her? He could just have told her some sob story about me and be using her as bait.

No one can make the choice for me. And I have no one to talk things over with. But I can try to find out as much as I can before making an irreversible decision.

"Alice, close Eyestream. Contact my father."

His avatar soon appears in the white room. Eva, Pieter, and Katrin are nowhere to be seen but I'm sure they're watching closely. They must suspect something's going on, but probably don't know what. I *hope* they don't know.

"Hello, son. How can I help?"

"I want you to tell me who Julia is."

"You know I can't do that, Manuel."

"She says she's my sister. Why would anyone do that?"

"We already discussed this. Whoever she is, she definitely isn't your sister."

"Then why am I so sure I know her and that I can trust her? And why are you trying so hard to keep her away from me?"

"That's not what we're trying to do."

"Really? Right after I contacted her, the connection cut and her

Nymochat account was deleted. The next time I saw her was in the park with your former business partner Marten Raffay. While I was trying to talk to her you cut the connection again. Then you took away the drone and car so I'll never be able to find them. Are you really telling me you aren't trying to keep me away from her?"

"It probably all looks really strange from your point of view, Manuel. But you don't know Marten. He wouldn't think twice about using a girl he knows you've fallen in love with."

"In love? Where did you get that idea?"

"It's the only explanation for why you're so anxious to see her again."

"That's ridiculous! I'm not in love with her! I just want to find out why I know her."

"You don't know her, Manuel. You just think you do. Your memory was badly damaged. You don't remember anyone from before. It's sad, but true."

I'm quiet for a bit, taking time to make my decision. Then I nod my computer-generated head.

"You're right. I don't remember anyone. I don't even know who you are. But I know you're not my father."

Eva's avatar appears in the room. "Manuel! How can you say such a thing?"

"Stay out of it, Eva. My father wouldn't try to keep me away from the only person in the world who could help me remember my past. He wouldn't stand in the way of me talking to Julia, he would encourage it."

"You know that's not true, Manuel," the psychologist argues. "You don't remember your past because your memory was irreparably damaged. Julia is a random girl who triggered a déjà vu experience."

"Well, if that's true, then there's no reason to stop me seeing her."

"There's Marten Raffay! He's using her! Can't you see that?"

"Then let me talk to Marten Raffay."

"No way!" the man who's supposed to be my father says. "He'll just pollute you with his paranoid delusions. He already has."

"Maybe we should let him talk to Marten," Eva says, bizarrely. "I don't think Raffay's going to make Manuel any more mistrustful than he already is."

"No. I won't allow it!" Henning Jaspers replies.

"Well, there's not much you can do to stop me," I say in my blank computer voice. "Cogito, ergo sum!"

"What?" asks the man who says he's my father.

There's no time to reply. A black circle appears in the luminous floor under my feet. It quickly gets bigger. And it isn't just a circle. It's a hole. An eddy pulls me in.

For a moment, I'm surrounded by pure darkness. Then it gets lighter and I see that I'm in a room. There's a desk and a stocky man with a beard: Marten Raffay. I see a panel in front me. Marten looks up and I realize that I'm looking at him through a 3D camera attached to his computer monitor. He's sitting in front of a bare brick wall with thick, embedded wooden beams. I see a field with cows through the window.

The camera doesn't move when I try to turn my head.

Julia walks into the frame. She leans over Marten's shoulder and stares at me. "Can he see us?" she says.

"Yes," Marten confirms.

"Hello, Manuel!" Julia says. "Can you hear me?"

"Yes," I answer.

I'm not sure how my voice is transmitted but Julia can hear me because she gives a huge smile even as her eyes fill with tears. "Is it really you?"

"I guess. I'm not really sure who I am."

"I have to admit I'm impressed," Marten says. "I thought it would take you longer to work out the code."

"To be honest, I'm not sure this is such a good idea," I reply. "My father says you just want to use me to get back at him."

"He's not your father, Manuel," Julia says. "Our parents died a long time ago."

"I've lost my memory. How do I know you're telling the truth? How can I be sure you're actually my sister?"

"Of course I'm your sister. And you *do* know, otherwise you wouldn't have activated Marten's program. Trust your instincts, Manuel!"

"What did Henning tell you about me?" Marten says.

"He said you used to be business partners, that you were a brilliant developer. That you started taking drugs and got paranoid so

- 121 -

he had to cut you off. That you're trying to get back at him and want to use me to do it. That you helped develop this simulation system and built in a back door, which his security team found. And that you may have killed my mother."

"Hmm. Smart. And how did he explain Julia?"

"As a sort of déjà vu caused by a brain malfunction, which makes me think I know her."

"What a pig!" Julia yells.

"Calm down, Julia. Like all good lies, it's pretty close to the truth. We were partners and we did build Dark Star together. As you see, the bit about the back door is also true, but his people only found part of my coding, the piece I wanted them to find; that's why we're able to talk right now. The bit about me taking drugs is true. But the thing about killing your mother is nonsense. Also, Henning Jaspers has never been married and doesn't have a son. He made that up so he'd have a reasonable explanation for why you're stuck in a virtual world with no memory."

"I'm really curious to hear *your* reasonable explanation for how that happened."

"Like I said, Henning and I set up Dark Star and it made us rich. But developing games wasn't enough. We collaborated to make better interfaces between humans and computers. We wanted to make people's experience of virtual worlds as real as possible. Then we had the idea to develop direct interfaces between brains and computers. The idea wasn't new and had already been used success-fully for medical research. We heard about amazing results that helped blind people regain their sight and paraplegics operate computers using only brainpower. We set up a research institute to study neurointerfaces, which is what we called them."

"And I was one of your patients?"

"I'm getting to you. The important thing is that our attitudes really began to diverge. I was more interested in the technology's potential for helping people with serious health issues. But Henning wanted something else. He wanted to create a virtual world that is so perfect you can't tell it apart from the real world. A bit like *The Matrix*."

"The film?"

"Yes, exactly. Have you watched it?"

"I'm not sure. I know what it's about, but I think I may have read about it somewhere."

"Anyway, Henning's real goal was to disconnect from the real world, to disconnect from his body and live a better life in a virtual world. He wanted to solve humanity's oldest challenge: He wanted to defeat death. Not even the most up-to-date medicine can increase a life span for as long as you like. Certain medical advances mean you could live to a hundred, or even a hundred and twenty. But Henning wanted to live a thousand years. At first I thought he was joking, but he was deadly serious."

"I still don't understand what that has to do with me."

"Hold on a second. You need to understand his rationale first. Some researchers claim that humans could pretty much live forever. The idea is you upload a perfect copy of their minds into a computer with a high enough capacity. But that's nonsense. Because that copy wouldn't be the same person, nothing you could even call a 'person.' 'How can that be a perfect copy of me if I'm standing here talking to it?' Henning said, and I had to agree with him. He also believed it would be impossible to create a perfect copy of a brain and all its complex inner workings, at least in his lifetime. I had to agree with him there too. So the only option for fulfilling his crazy plan and prolonging his life would be to keep his brain alive."

"And how does that work?"

"Like all body organs, the brain degenerates with age, and may develop conditions like dementia. But some doctors are convinced that, in principle, it has a much longer shelf life than other organs, like the heart, say. Henning believes that if he can completely disconnect the brain from the body and supply it with durable or easily replaceable artificial body parts, then his plan might work, at least in theory. And he's determined to do exactly that. He's obsessed with the idea of immortality."

"Immortality? Didn't you just say he wanted to live to a thousand?"

"He's hoping that during those thousand years technology would advance to the stage where he could extend his life for another thousand years, and so on. In his mind there's no limit to how long he could live. It's not entirely implausible if you look at how far technology has developed in just the last fifty years."

"Still sounds pretty far-fetched."

"It's a massive technological challenge, of course. And that's where we grew apart. As far as I was concerned, anything we did had to be with the full consent of the people involved; it had to be legal and follow ethical guidelines. But Henning said that would stop him from moving forward quickly. He's probably right. So he started running illegal experiments. He put neurointerfaces into patients' brains without their knowledge. There were side effects and rejection reactions. There was nearly a scandal—a patient was about to sue, but we paid him off. And that gave Henning the idea to just pay people to agree to his experiments."

"Who would be a guinea pig just for cash?" I say, but then I turn cold and answer my own question. "You don't put yourself under the knife, you sign someone else up. Julia, you said our parents died a long time ago. Does that mean we're adopted?"

Her expression is dark. "Yes, we are. Our adoptive parents are a couple from Norderstedt with no biological children. He's called Ralph, a lawyer, his wife, Birte, runs a dog-grooming salon. They were okay parents, but lived beyond their means and came unstuck. Plus there were your epileptic fits. When Henning Jaspers said he could cure you and that they'd even get paid, they couldn't sign the paperwork fast enough. I had no idea. Just thought he was some generous millionaire who wanted to help. I only realized things were off when they stopped me from visiting you at the clinic. But what could I do? Nothing. Then Iris came along and told me some-one had approached her, that someone called Manuel wanted to contact me. When you wrote to me on Nymochat I still couldn't believe it was you."

"Iris is LittleDevil?"

"Yes. LittleDevil is her Eyestream name."

"Did she tell you that Pieter gave her two hundred euros so she'd give him your Nymochat name?"

"What? No! Actually, it doesn't matter. I'm glad she did. The connection died and after that you didn't get in touch again."

"Your Nymochat account was deleted."

"What? It's working fine."

"They filter and manipulate what you see online," Marten explains. "Being able to hide or adulterate what you see is child's play."

Of course. That explains why I suddenly couldn't find LittleDevil and July2001. And the fake internet reports about the attack against my fictitious mother and me. Assuming Julia and Raffay are telling the truth.

"Anyway, I kept feeling something wasn't right," Julia says quickly. "I tried to talk to our adoptive parents, but they wouldn't listen. Then I began researching Henning Jaspers. I discovered Marten had left the company under a cloud and decided to get in touch. When I told him what had happened he knew straightaway you were my brother. My brother who was being held captive and experimented on by that pig! We thought you might try to get back in touch, so kept going back to the same spot in City Park where you first saw me. I wasn't very hopeful, but it was all we had. You were smart, that's why it worked. As soon as I saw the drone, I knew it was you. I don't know why, but I just knew."

"Why didn't you go to the police?"

"It's not that simple," Marten explains. "To the outside world, Henning Jaspers helps people. Your adoptive parents gave him written consent to perform surgery on you. Proving he's carrying out unethical experiments would involve a complex legal process, which his lawyers could easily drag out. Without consent from your direct relatives, it would take years to get an assessor anywhere near you, and your adoptive parents *are* your direct relatives—and he's paid them off. As for me—well, I actually was convicted for drug possession and did go to rehab. That somewhat reduces my credibility as a witness."

"Don't we have any other relatives?

"Dad was from Puerto Rico," Julia explains. "We might still have family there, but I don't know them and, even if we did, they can't do much here. Mom was an only child. Her parents both died too, otherwise they could have taken care of us when we were kids."

"How did our parents die?"

"In a car accident. They were both drunk. She was driving."

"You mean, there's no one who can help us? There's nothing we can do?"

"Oh, I never said that! We'll get you out."

CHAPTER 16

"What happened?" Henning Jaspers says. "You just disappeared."

He's standing next to me in the white room. The walls are blank, apart from the one that now has a door in it. Henning can't see it, but I can. And I'm the only one who can open it.

"How should I know?" I say. "Everything went black. I was pretty scared, as you can imagine. It was like being buried alive." My computer voice still doesn't really show my feelings, so it's easy to hide the lies Marten and I spoke about.

He looks at me for a second. "I don't know what you've done, son, but I'm really worried you may just have put yourself in serious danger."

"I didn't do anything."

"Don't lie! You're forgetting we're constantly monitoring your brain waves. You're hooked to the world's most powerful lie detector. Tell me the truth."

"Or?"

He sighs. "Manuel, this isn't a game. It's deadly serious. Marten Raffay wants to get back at me. I don't know what lies he's told you, but they must have been pretty convincing if you believe him over your own father."

"You're not my father," I say.

"How can you say that?" he yells. "How could you ever say such a thing, Manuel! After everything I've done! Everything I've been through! We stood at your mother's graveside together— remember that?"

"I remember standing at a graveside. I just don't believe it was my mother's grave."

"I won't listen to any more of this! I don't know how Marten's managed to turn your head and I'm really hurt you'd believe him over me. But I won't put up with this! I'll make sure he leaves us in peace. Until then, you're safe here. Sorry, Manuel, but for now I'm withdrawing all your privileges. You won't get to browse the internet. You can play computer games, watch films, read ebooks, but from now on you'll have absolutely no contact with the outside world. We're going to have to review all our systems. It could take weeks, months even. And it would really help if you told us how he managed to contact you. The more you help, the more likely I am to let you back on the internet. Maybe I'll even let you talk to Julia. But she isn't your sister so I'd have to get her to realize that she has to stop lying to you. Marten was probably using her. Who knows, maybe you'll even become friends."

I say nothing. The fact that this man is using Julia to try and get me on his side is all the proof I need. I've done the right thing.

"All right, up to you," he says. "Your choice. I just hope it doesn't take you too long to realize it's the wrong choice. Bye, son."

"Bye."

His avatar disappears and Pieter's pops up a short while later.

"Hi, Manuel. What's going on? Your father's really upset."

"He's not my father."

"What? Why do you say that?"

"Not important. Leave me alone!"

"Listen, I'm not sure what's going on here, kid. But I'm on your side."

"You work for the man who says he's my father. What's the expression? A dog won't bite the hand that feeds it."

"It's not that. I'm freelance, an independent contractor. I can't afford to be picky about what my clients do, but we have our own code of ethics. We're hired hands, sure, but we don't kill innocent people unless there's no choice."

"*Unless there's no choice.* That sounds like a pretty fluid code of ethics."

"Maybe. But I like you. You're in a bad place. If I find out some-one's using you, no matter who it is, I'll be on your side. You need to know that."

"And you're telling me this while he's listening?"

"Your father's on the phone with his lawyer."

- 130 -

"Save it, Pieter. I enjoyed spending time with you. But I'm on my own now. Please leave."

"If that's how you want it. Good luck, Manuel."

No sooner has he left than Eva's avatar shows up. Can't they just let it rest?

"Piss off!"

"Manuel, I just wanted to say you're making a huge mistake. It's really hard to build trust, but it can be broken in a matter of seconds. Maybe your father will calm down if you apologize and tell him the truth. Otherwise I don't know where this will lead. He pays a huge amount to keep you alive and give you the luxury of your virtual world."

Luxury? That's the limit!

"Thanks for the advice, my dear Eva. I'll have to think really hard about that one. Oh, okay, I've thought about it: piss off!"

She leaves without saying a word.

Eva's overt warning is unnerving. She's right, of course: Henning Jaspers could just turn off the machines that are keeping me alive. Then he'd just tell my adoptive parents some sob story about how he did everything he could to save me, and hand over cash to make sure they believe him. *Game over.*

But is that a good enough reason to stop? No way! What kind of life would that be? To live so that Henning can do random experiments on me? Anyway, I'm expendable. He'll get rid of me when I'm no longer needed. I'd rather die now.

I wait awhile to see if they'll send someone else to talk me around to the idea that my so-called father is the good guy and that Marten Raffay is the villain. But it looks like they've finished telling tall tales.

So I open the door in the white wall and walk through.

The room next door is smaller and looks like some kind of command center. Instead of massive screens covering all four walls, there's a block of monitors arranged across one wall. The middle screen is bigger than the rest. There's a panel with buttons, a keyboard, an old-fashioned telephone, and an office chair. The floor is made of gray plastic, and the walls are gray too. Framed pictures hang here and there. They're of me as a child with an older girl—Julia, unmistakably. I'm so relieved to see her. Of course, the pictures could just be photoshopped, but my connection to Julia feels absolutely real. I can trust her, I just know it.

One of the pictures shows my adoptive parents. The people who sold me to Henning Jaspers smile happily into the camera, holding their six- and eight-year-old adopted children. I should probably feel angry, but couldn't care less.

But I do care about the woman in white in one of the other pictures. I immediately recognize her as the mysterious woman I've seen before. Is she my real mother? If so, it's a long time since she died. Eva's right about one thing: My subconscious mind probably projected her face onto the heads of strangers as a way to keep her memory alive.

I look at the monitors. They show an array of images taken by cameras installed inside and outside Henning Jaspers's luxury villa. One shows the meeting room where he, Pieter, Eva, and a fat man in a badly fitting suit are now sitting around the big table. The panel has buttons that allow me to change the picture on the big monitor. I select the image on the monitor showing the conference room and listen in.

"... said it was a mistake," the man in the suit ends. He has an unusually high-pitched voice for a man. "Who knows what havoc the hacker might have caused."

"I thought you said the system was completely secure," Henning Jaspers says.

"Against outside threats, but not internal ones. That's impossible to do."

"Manuel has no way to access the system," Eva interjects. "How could he threaten it?"

"I don't know. Anyway, it was a zero-day exploit."

"A what?" Pieter says.

"A new software error. Raffay must have detected it, and I suppose he got the boy to exploit it."

"And then?"

"Raffay took control of the system so he could talk to the boy without us monitoring the conversation. As soon as I realized, I shut down, then restarted the simulation software. That cut the connection and now the system's back to normal." The fat man rubs his chin nervously.

"And you're sure Raffay can't contact him anymore?" Jaspers asks.

"Yes. Like I said, I immediately discovered the secure connection to outside and shut it down. If it happens again, I'll know right away." He holds up a small tablet, which must be what he uses to control the villa's security system.

"Might he have installed malware that can manipulate our system?" Jaspers barks. "After all, he built in a back door before."

"We found that and made it secure."

"But what if there's another back door?"

"No. We checked thoroughly."

"Can the boy reactivate the connection to outside?" Jaspers wants to know.

"Unlikely," the man says. "Our security system is self-learning. It won't get caught out twice in the same way. I'll admit it was a serious malfunction, but all that happened is Raffay got to talk to the boy uninterrupted for a few minutes."

"*All* that happened?" Eva says. "Who knows what he said to Manuel?"

"The truth, probably," Pieter says dryly.

"Either way, he's a lot more difficult to handle now," the psychologist says. "At this rate, it'll be almost impossible to get meaningful test results."

Test results. It sounds so harmless—so cold-blooded. That's all I am to them—a lab rat.

"What do you suggest?" Jaspers asks.

"I don't know yet. But I've got a bad feeling. We still have no idea how Raffay hacked into our system. We should focus on finding out."

"I agree," the security guy says.

"None of this makes any sense," Pieter says. "Why should Raffay go to so much trouble just to talk to Manuel for a few minutes? He must have done more than that. He must have found some way to install malware. We should take down the whole system and reinstall it."

"Are you insane, Pieter?" the security guy says. "If we do that, everything will be unsecured. That's exactly what he wants and most likely why he spoke to Manuel: He wants to get in and asked the boy to find out about our security measures."

"That's ridiculous!" Eva says. "Why would he do that?"

"Isn't that obvious? He wants to take the boy."

"I think Mr. Hellms is right," Jaspers says. "Raffay wants the boy. He wants his help to prove we're conducting illegal experiments. If he succeeds, we're finished."

"Bring it on!" Pieter replies. "I'll sort out Raffay."

"He might not come alone," Eva says.

"So what. This house is a fortress. No one can get in."

"I agree!" the big guy says. "So long as we're not dumb enough to shut down the security software."

"Still," Eva says. "Let's assume he finds some way to take the boy. What can he do? Who would believe him?"

"No one would believe anything Raffay says," Jaspers agrees. "Except Manuel's sister . . . and Manuel!"

Eva turns to another man seated at the table, who's been listening so silently and stilly that I'd barely registered his presence until now. He has a worried look on his face. "Dr. Friese, could you perform another procedure to make him forget the events of the last few days?"

I feel my skin crawl, even though I know it must be an illusion. They're not just feeding me lies—they literally wipe the truth from my memory!

"That's tricky," the doctor answers. "And it wouldn't make much difference. He'll get his memory back as soon as the bioelectrical impulse inhibitors are deactivated. Once he's out of our control, Manuel will gradually remember everything."

"Then make sure his memories are permanently deleted," Jaspers orders.

"How can I do that?" the doctor says. "You expect me to perform a lobotomy?"

"If necessary. Whatever it takes; under no circumstances must the boy get his memory back. He can't ever be in a position to testify against us!"

"The procedure would cause permanent brain damage. I can't do that."

Jaspers stares at him coldly. "My dear Dr. Friese," he says with fake kindness. "Surely I don't need to remind you that you owe me an awful lot of money? If we're caught you'll be ruined and lose your license to practice. You'll probably end up in prison. You're part of this, whether you like it or not. So please spare us your morals! You'll operate on the boy as soon as possible, and if he's a drooling moron afterward, then that's our bad luck and we'll just have to start again from scratch. Until then he absolutely cannot be in touch with Raffay. That's the end of the discussion. Friese, prepare the operation. Hellms, you're responsible for securing the house. Pieter, make preparations in case someone tries to enter the premises. If Raffay really does show up here, make sure he never leaves, and make it look like self-defense. Can you do that?"

Pieter nods. Weirdly enough, I feel disappointed. Did I actually believe he was my friend?

"Eva, stay with Dr. Friese to keep an eye on the boy," Jaspers orders. "I want to know if he has anything else up his sleeve. Let's get to work!"

CHAPTER 17

can't quite believe Julia and Marten Raffay can get me out of this secure prison. Even so, I cling to the hope like a drowning man clutching driftwood. And something the doctor said gives my hope an irrational edge: *He'll get his memory back as soon as the bioelectrical impulse inhibitors are deactivated. Once he's out of our control, Manuel will gradually remember everything.*

I could get my past back. And be myself again. Maybe lead a normal life, until one day the white room and everything that happened here is just a distant memory, a hazy nightmare. However unlikely that is, the possibility has to be worth trying for. But there isn't much time. Dr. Friese is probably already prepping the surgery that will totally wipe my memory. I pick up the telephone receiver. It buzzes a couple of times, then Marten Raffay picks up.

"We have to hurry!" I blurt out, then tell him what I overheard.

"Scum!" Marten rages. "Right, we'll bring things forward. It's five thirty p.m. The earliest we can be there is around eleven. Let's hope Friese takes longer than that to get things ready."

We discuss the plan. I have time to familiarize myself with the security system—the simulated panel in front of me is an exact replica of the one Hellms is using. I see everything he sees, and can manipulate what appears on his monitors. But I have to be careful: He mustn't realize the system's been hijacked, otherwise it's all over.

A total of twenty-two CCTV cameras feed into the security system—nine inside the house, thirteen outside, around the gate and perimeter wall. They're all connected to a software program that automatically identifies and flags any unauthorized access. But I can intercept that notification.

The system has loads of blind spots. There are no cameras on the top floor. There are only four on the ground floor: one at the entrance, one in each corridor to the left and right of the hall, and one in the fireplace room where the meeting was held. The basement has cameras in the garage, swimming pool, fitness room, and two in the corridors. The medical wing, which is where I'm being held, isn't monitored. I find that strange. Pieter didn't show me that area during our tour of the house either.

All this means I can't properly monitor the inside of the house but have a good view of the gardens and nearby roads. The villa stands on a low hill. The back section of the garden is on a gentle slope. Mature beech and oak trees shade a small lily pond and the barbecue area. At the front, there's a small outdoor pool and a lawn ringed with rhododendron bushes. A ten-foot wall secures the property. There are metal spikes on top of the wall, which makes it hard to climb over. The only way onto the property is down two wide driveways behind automatic gates, and a side door for pedestrians. The neighboring villas have just as much security even though they're not as big or opulent.

To mislead anyone watching me, I leave a full season of *Doctor Who* playing on one of the white room walls. My avatar is standing in front of it, transfixed. Hopefully Eva and Friese will think I'm trying to relax.

It's already getting dark outside when the phone finally rings a little after eleven.

"We're ready," Raffay says. "Where are they all?"

"Hellms is in the security room," I reply. "Pieter is watching football in the living room. Eva is in my fath—I mean, Jaspers's office."

"Can you hear what they're saying?"

"No. There's no security camera in his office and I can't hear anything from the corridor."

"Where's the doctor?"

"In the medical wing, I guess."

"You guess?"

"I haven't seen him since the meeting. He went down to the basement and disappeared."

"Are you sure he's still in the house?"

"No, but I haven't seen him come out."

"Okay. I'm activating my camera glasses now." Suddenly one of the gray-painted walls lights up. I see the world from Marten's point of view. He's sitting at the wheel of a car, driving through the lamplit residential streets.

"Is the picture ready?" he asks.

"Yes. Where's Julia?"

"I'm here!"

Marten turns to face her. She's in the passenger seat wearing a black coverall and a sort of ski mask, which make her look like something out of a bad action movie.

"Could you be any more obvious?" I say.

"Hold on, I'm turning my camera on now." Another wall fills with Julia's view. I can see Marten now. He's wearing jeans, a sweatshirt, and a baseball cap.

"We'll be there soon," he says. A short while later, I see the wall of Jaspers's property, and one of the monitors shows a dark delivery truck appear on the southwest corner. I make out Marten's sweatshirt and baseball cap.

"You're on camera seventeen."

"Okay."

Marten drives past, takes the next turn, and parks. He gets out and walks back to Jaspers's property while Julia climbs into the back of the truck. I wonder what she's doing but don't ask because we agreed to speak as little as possible once our plan was underway. So I silently watch Marten get into a Mercedes he parked within sight of camera seventeen earlier. He drives around the corner, changes vehicles, then drives the delivery truck around and parks in the space he's just freed up. All that shows on camera seventeen is one car driving off and another taking its place. Nothing unusual there.

"It's your turn, Manuel!" Marten gets out of the car, crosses the road, and disappears out of view.

I wait until the road is clear, then freeze camera seventeen's frame and feed it into the security system. Marten left an instruction book on my panel complete with a virtual ring binder that showed me how to do this. If Hellms looks really closely, he might notice that nothing on camera seventeen is moving—not even the leaves on the trees. If he's observant he might realize that the cars driving across camera sixteen don't go past camera seventeen. But because there are fewer monitors than there are cameras, the pictures from outside only come up in a regular sequence. So it's hard to spot that kind of anomaly—it's a security weakness Marten picked up on.

"Done?" he says.

"Yes. But hurry. At some point Hellms will notice something's not right."

I watch through Marten's camera as he walks back to the truck and climbs into the back, where Julia's waiting. He changes into a dark coverall with a ski mask, then unloads an aluminum ladder. There are no other cars in sight so he leans the ladder against the wall and quickly climbs up. He puts down a sort of saddle with narrow slats on either side that cover the metal spikes, so he can stand on the wall ledge. Julia goes up next. She's just climbing the ladder when a car drives past. She flinches and I tense, but the driver hasn't noticed anything. Or anyway, the car doesn't stop.

Once Julia has climbed to the top of the wall, Marten quickly pulls up the ladder, then uses it to climb down the other side. Less than thirty seconds later, they're crouching in the shadows of the wall.

I deactivate the floodlights near the house. When the cameras detect movement they normally switch on automatically and light up the garden like a football stadium. Next, I change the freeze-frame images on the security cameras while Marten and Julia make their way across the garden. Suddenly I have an idea. I type in a few commands and save the images I've just frozen.

"Where are they now?" Marten says as they reach the southwest corner of the house. That's where the meeting room with the fireplace is—it has a door that leads onto the garden.

"Eva's gone to her room, which is next to the fireplace room. Pieter's in the living room; you should be able to see him."

"Yes, I see him."

"Jaspers is in the swimming pool. He might use the sauna before going to bed."

"That man has nerves of steel! What about Hellms?"

"He's still in the security room. Probably trying to work out how you broke into the system."

"He can try. Hellms is an idiot."

"Let's hope so."

"Quiet now. We're going in."

I watch through Marten's camera glasses as he runs toward the patio door that leads into the fireplace room. The light is on in Eva's room. There's a blue-tinged flicker—the television is on. That's good.

Marten takes out a glass cutter. The door is double-glazed so he has to cut two holes. It sounds really loud through his mic, but Eva and Pieter don't seem to hear. He finally finishes and opens the door. I block the alert to the security system that signals when the door is being opened, and put a freeze-frame picture on camera nine, inside the fireplace room.

Julia has been watching from a hiding place behind a shrub. She ventures out and runs toward Marten. They quietly enter the house and listen at the door that leads onto the corridor.

"Show a freeze-frame picture on the corridor camera," Marten says.

"No, I have a better idea," I say. "Just wait there a second."

"What are you doing?" Julia asks.

"No time to explain. Trust me."

A second later a shrill alarm sounds.

CHAPTER 18

"What's happening?" Pieter asks. I hear his voice through the camera in the corridor—I'm picking everything up through the security system.

"Someone's in the grounds!" Hellms yells, his voice cracking with anxiety. "In the southwest corner of the property, behind the pond!"

I watch Pieter on camera three, which monitors the back of the house and part of the garden near the wall. He's standing by the bay window in the living room and staring out over the floodlit garden, wearing a headset and carrying a small gun in his right hand.

"Are you sure? I don't see anything."

"Of course I'm sure. I saw them clearly, right behind the bushes. Go and look!"

"Okay." Pieter steps onto the terrace. He slowly heads to the pond. "Where are they?"

"Don't know. Can't see them anymore."

"And you're sure it wasn't just a cat?"

"Ever seen a cat in a black coverall and a ski mask?"

"How many of them were there?"

"At least two."

Pieter takes a couple more steps forward, then stops in the middle of the lawn.

I activate the emergency locking mechanism. Heavy metal shutters drop down in front of the windows.

Pieter spins around. "Hellms, you idiot!" he yells into his headset. "What are you doing?"

"N-nothing!" the head of security stammers. "The system must have automatically activated the emergency locking mechanism."

Pieter runs back to the house, but by the time he reaches the terrace, everything is locked. "Open up, right now!"

"I'm trying!" Hellms yells. "For some reason the system isn't responding!"

"Damn it . . ." Pieter mutters. I don't hear anything else because Hellms has cut the conversation.

That solves one problem.

"What did you do?" Marten asks. "You've alerted the whole house! Now everyone knows we're here!"

"I've locked Pieter out. He's the most dangerous. Quiet!"

I monitor the corridor camera and watch Eva leave her room and run into the living room. "Pieter? What the hell's going on? Pieter!"

She looks around, then goes back into the corridor outside her room. Hopefully she'll go back in . . . No, she's going into the fireplace room!

I still have time to shout: "Watch out!"

A second later the lights in the fireplace room turn on. I see Eva's shocked expression through Marten's camera glasses. "What . . . who . . ."

Marten holds up his gun. "Quiet!" he says. "We don't want to hurt anyone. We just want Manuel!"

The psychologist raises her hands. "This is nothing to do with me," she stammers. "I was always against the experiments! Honestly!"

"Shut up!" Marten orders.

"I can help you get the boy out," Eva says. "I know where he is. Come, I'll show you."

"Don't trust her!" I warn him.

"Don't worry," Marten replies. He points the gun toward the corridor and Eva's room. "In there!"

She reluctantly goes into the guest room. Marten gives Julia the gun.

"Hold this. Shoot if you have to. The gun doesn't have a safety catch. Just pull the trigger."

"Oh, don't worry, I can manage that," Julia says coldly. Marten ties Eva's hands behind her back with cable ties.

"Ow! You're hurting me!"

"Just pray we don't do to you what you did to my brother, you viper!" Julia says.

"Quiet!" Marten urges. He uses a small towel from the en suite bathroom to gag the struggling psychologist, and then straps her legs to the bed using more cable ties.

While they restrain Eva, I take care of Hellms. I can't see him because there's no camera in the security room, but I can tell from my virtual panel that he's desperately trying to change the system settings.

But Marten's system hack means I control *all* the automated systems on Jaspers's property. That means I can activate the self-drive car in the garage, so I rev the engine a couple of times. And open the garage door. Just as I'd hoped, Hellms appears on camera ten, which monitors the small basement corridor, the door to the security room, and the garage door. He's holding a gun and listening at the door. I rev the engine one more time.

Hellms types a six-figure number into the keypad next to the door. It releases. He pulls the door open, grabs his gun in both hands, and points it into the dark garage.

I drive the car out through the garage door.

"Stop!" Hellms shouts, running after it.

"Quick, go to the basement!" I tell Marten. "You have to close the garage door! Hurry!" I direct them down the basement stairs, along the corridor, and into the garage. Marten gets there just as Hellms realizes he should have stayed inside the house.

Hellms points his gun. "Hey! Hands up or—"

Marten slams the garage door in his face. I watch on CCTV as the head of security frantically types numbers into the outside keypad. But it's no use, because I've already changed the door code.

"Good job, Manuel!" Marten says. "Now we just need to take

care of Henning Jaspers and the doctor. Where are they? And more importantly, where are you?"

"I have no idea," I reply. "The last time I saw Jaspers he was in the swimming pool. Friese hasn't showed up anywhere yet."

"Okay. Let's check the security room first." Marten goes into the room Hellms had come out of. The panel really does look exactly like my virtual version, even down to the way the monitors are laid out on the wall. Everything is covered in biscuit crumbs and dirty coffee cups. There's a duvet in the corner—Hellms must sometimes spend the night here.

Marten scans the monitors but neither Jaspers nor Friese are anywhere in sight. The outdoor security cameras show Hellms and Pieter deep in conversation. Pieter looks like he's about to throttle Hellms.

Julia rummages through the drawers under the panel. She pulls out a folder and flicks through. "Look at this!" she says, holding up a stack of floor plans inside a plastic folder. They're an architect's drawings of the house.

Marten and Julia lean over the drawings in such a way that I can see them too. The plans for this floor show the swimming pool, sauna, fitness room, garage, boiler room, wine cellar, and the security room, labeled STORAGE ROOM. And that's it.

"Where's the room with Manuel in it?" Julia asks.

Marten doesn't answer. Instead, he goes out into the main corridor and opens the boiler room door. Through his glasses, I see a modern gas heating system, a steel distribution panel secured with a padlock, pipes, and cables on walls, and a shelf with cleaning products and tools. As you'd expect, the wine cellar is full of wine racks, but nothing else. Marten glances into the fitness room Pieter and my father used when they visited the virtual world. Then he draws his pistol, listens against the swimming pool door, and yanks it open.

It's dark. Light streams in through the glass panel on the left. There are a couple of loungers next to the sauna at the back. The room is empty; the surface of the water is flat. There are no wet footprints. No one has swum here recently.

Marten walks over to the sauna, opens the wooden door, and looks in. That's empty too, and so is the small shower cubicle.

"You're sure that the last time you saw Jaspers was when he went to the swimming pool?" he says.

"Yes. But he may have left without me noticing. I can't watch all of the CCTV cameras at the same time."

"Maybe he's—" Marten starts, but he's cut off by a loud bang. "What was that?"

I frantically search the monitors. There's another loud bang and this time I see what's happening.

"It's Pieter. He's got an ax—he's trying to break down the steel shutters outside the living room. Hurry!"

"Is there any way you can slow him down?" Marten says.

"I'll try."

I scroll through the menus on my control panel until I find something that might work. Meanwhile, Pieter pounds the shutters like a madman. Hellms is next to him, watching. So far, Pieter's only dented the metal, but sooner or later he'll get through. We're running out of time.

Marten systematically scours the wall to the right of the swimming pool. "There has to be a hidden door here or something."

"We could ask the psychologist?" Julia suggests.

"You think she'll tell us where Manuel is?"

"If we give her a reason to." I don't like how she says that. Would Julia use torture to get me out? I find the possibility quite disturbing.

"She'll probably send us the wrong way so we just waste time," Marten says. The house reverberates with the sound of Pieter's ax. "You heard Manuel: We have to hurry. Help me look."

By now, I've managed to activate the self-drive lawn mower. It looks like a giant ladybug as I drive it onto the terrace. When Hellms sees the machine he panics and runs off screaming. But Pieter doesn't react and just keeps on pounding the metal. He only steps aside when I aim the lawn mower at his legs.

"You really think a garden tool's going to stop me, Raffay?" He slams the ax into the lawn mower but doesn't cause any damage. I reverse to get another run at him, but Pieter steps to one side, grabs the machine, and flips it onto its back so that the rotating blades and drive wheels spin helplessly in the air. Then he turns to the window. One of the shutters is showing a small tear. They won't hold off Pieter's unrelenting attack for much longer.

CHAPTER 19

The blows from Pieter's ax keep slamming the house. Marten, Julia, and I have no idea where I'm being held. The idea that I could be somewhere completely different, maybe in a nearby house, or even in another city, slowly dawns on me. Marten and Julia's desperate plan is going to fail.

"You have to leave, right now!" I say. "Pieter is doing everything to force his way through the shutters. If he manages to get into the house he'll kill you, for sure."

"No way!" Julia says. "I'm not leaving you here!"

"But we don't actually know I am *here*."

"You are here. I know it!" She leans over the edge of the pool, looking for a hidden mechanism below the waterline. In the meantime, Marten goes back into the sauna.

A terrible crunching sound tells us Pieter has finally managed to break through the shutters. It'll be a matter of minutes before he's in the house. One armed, experienced, and very angry mercenary against a teenager and a computer programmer. Marten may have a gun, but that won't mean much.

Pieter is using the ax handle to crowbar open the shutters. I have to do something! I look at the lawn mower lying helplessly on its back like an upturned turtle. The idea was good but its execution could have been better.

So I steer the self-drive SUV straight through the flowering rhododendron bushes, turn onto the lawn near the pond, and open the throttle. The wheels spin and for a second the car doesn't move at all, but then it goes into gear and careens forward. It only manages to reach a speed of 12 mph, but it's a heavy car with enough power to squash Pieter like a bug.

The South African turns. Ax in hand, he stares at the car like a cowboy preparing for a gunfight, but he doesn't budge.

I yell when the car is a few yards away from the house wall, even though I know he can't hear me. "Pieter, get out of the way!" He doesn't react and I do an emergency stop. But the tires are caked in grass and dirt and the car slides across the terrace like it's on an ice rink.

Right at the last minute, Pieter jumps forward and lands on the hood just as the car crashes into the steel shutters. Luckily, the force of the crash doesn't break them open. I reverse, assuming that Pieter will jump off and keep working on the shutters, which are now even more vulnerable. But I've underestimated him. He jumps, grabs the balcony rail above the terrace, and pulls himself up, ax gripped between his legs. Once there, he systematically pounds the lock on the balcony door. I park the car a few yards away and leave the motor running so Pieter knows I'll attack if he dares come back down. But he ignores me and keeps working at the balcony door. All I've done is gain some time.

"What's going on up there, Manuel?" Marten asks.

"I had a little run-in with Pieter."

"You? How?"

"I threatened him with the self-drive car and may have bought us some extra time. But hurry anyway."

"I think I've found something." Marten points at the sauna stove. It's filled with lava stone. The slick control panel has a temperature dial and a row of buttons numbered from one to nine.

"What?" Julia says.

"The control panel isn't normal. I don't often go to the sauna, but I've never seen a stove with nine heat settings. Maybe it's a keypad and we need to press the buttons in some particular order to operate a hidden mechanism."

"Yeah, right. And what code would that be?" Julia asks.

"Manuel, can you help us out here?"

"Try 287669." That was the code Hellms used for the door into the garage. Each door could have its own code, but it's entirely possible that Jaspers only wanted to have one number to remember.

Marten presses the buttons. There's a buzz and the back wall of the sauna slides open. There's a stairwell with steps leading down.

"Bingo!" Julia says.

"Careful! Jaspers and the doctor are probably down there and may already know you're coming."

"Probably," Marten agrees. He raises his pistol and goes down eight steps into a short corridor. There's a steel door on the right. Marten listens against the door, then opens it quietly. A dazzling light streams into the corridor. The room is full of machines. There are four monitors on a desk showing curves, diagrams, and rows of numbers. Shelves to the left and right are crammed with dozens of units with flashing lights. A glass window looks into another room, which is also brightly lit—it's clearly an operating theater.

Dr. Friese is sitting at the desk and staring at the monitors. He spins around when he hears the door open and jumps out of his chair in shock.

"What . . . who are you? What do you want?"

Marten walks in and turns the gun on the doctor.

"Stay calm. I don't want to hurt you!"

Dr. Friese raises his hands, taking a step back. He nods toward the glass window. "He's in there!"

Marten turns to face the window, which means I can see through the glass. There's a big steel table in the center of the room, complicated gadgets everywhere. A series of robot arms are attached to a rack in the ceiling. Their tips end in borers, scalpels, and scissors.

The naked body of a young man lies on the table. His head is clean-shaven. Bundles of cables protrude from his skull, leading into machines next to the table. The young man's face is covered in bandages. Cables poke out of the bandages too.

I can't believe that's me lying there, abused and mistreated. I feel like crying with rage and confusion, but my body can't do that. Jaspers is standing next to the table. He's wearing a white gown and holding one hand against my neck to check my pulse.

When Julia sees me she shouts and rips open the interconnecting door. Then she suddenly stops in the doorway. Jaspers has something in his hand: a syringe full of a greenish liquid. The needle is already piercing my neck.

I know it's impossible, but I feel the point in my neck. Marten holds up his gun and points it at Marten's head. "Leave the boy alone, Henning!"

"Hello, Marten," Jaspers replies, unmoved. "Put that ridiculous gun away and let's talk like grown-ups!"

"Move your hand away from the boy's neck first!"

"And give up my only advantage? Why would I do that? You're the intruders, not me!"

"Leave him alone!" Julia shouts. "Move away from Manuel or I'll—"

"Stay where you are, or your brother's dead! Just one drop of this nerve agent in his bloodstream and he'll never wake up!"

The sound of Pieter's muffled ax blows reaches us from upstairs. It's obvious that Jaspers is playing for time. He wants to stall Marten and Julia until Pieter arrives. Maybe he's bluffing and the syringe is full of a harmless sedative. Or maybe not.

"Let us take him, and we'll leave you alone," Marten says. "We won't go to the police. We have better things to do than tussle with your team of bloodthirsty lawyers."

"Do you really think I would take your word for that? You already betrayed me once, Marten!"

"I didn't betray you. You're the one that wanted to carry out illegal experiments."

"I wasn't forcing you to take part."

"No. But you knew I couldn't stand by and watch you misuse the technology I developed!"

"New scientific breakthroughs are always rejected and mis-understood. I'm working on making people immortal!"

"What you're doing is madness, and you're literally walking over dead bodies to do it!"

Something shatters upstairs. I have to do something!

"I don't have to justify myself to you," Jaspers says. "The kid's parents have consented to me testing new technologies on him. What I'm doing is totally legal. You, however, have broken into my house. You've poisoned the boy's sister with your paranoid ideas and made her follow you here. You've—"

One of the robotic arms has a small rotating bone saw in its tip. It shoots across the room and slices Jaspers's thumb with surgical precision. Blood spurts. The syringe drops to the ground. Jaspers screams, holding his mutilated hand against his chest.

"How did you do that, Manuel?" Marten asks. "I didn't think you could control this part of the system."

"It wasn't me," I say. "I didn't do it."

Dr. Friese walks into the room. "Sorry to resort to such drastic measures, Mr. Jaspers. But you left me no choice. Don't worry; they can reattach your thumb at the hospital. It'll only leave a small scar."

"You parasite!" Jaspers shouts, his white coat staining red. "You'll regret this! I'll finish you, Friese!"

"You already have," the doctor replies. "You tempted me with money, until I betrayed all the ideals I ever had. I've performed experiments on this boy, operated on his brain, and probably caused him irreparable damage. I'll spend the rest of my life in prison for that. I can't sink any lower. But I won't stand by and watch you commit murder!"

"Your life is over if Pieter catches you!"

"Shut up, Henning, or *your* life will be over!" Marten threatens.

"Just kill him!" Julia yells. "The shithead deserves it!"

"No," I say. "Don't stoop to his level, Julia!"

My sister picks up the syringe. "If he moves an inch, I'll use this!" Jaspers turns chalk white and slumps forward, groaning.

"Sort him out," Marten tells Dr. Friese. "We don't want to lose him."

"Manuel's our priority!" Julia insists. "We need to get away from here as quickly as possible!"

"You can't move him," the doctor says. "He's too weak. Unhooking him from the life support systems could kill him."

"If he stays here, Jaspers and that mercenary will kill him for sure!" Julia says. "We have to try!"

"All right. If you're sure." Dr. Friese flips switches on the machines next to the operating table.

Everything turns black. The virtual room with the security panel disappears, and so do the pictures of Marten and Julia. I can't see, hear, or feel anything.

I want to scream—but can't.

CHAPTER 20

First comes the pain.

It starts off dull, almost pleasant, like a blanket. But the blanket gets heavier and weighs me down. The pain is searing, like something's gnawing at me, tearing, pounding.

I want to scream but my throat and lungs feel like they're filled with burning coals. I try to open my eyes. Bright lights glare into my pupils, burn my retinas. I slam my eyes shut, and feel something I've missed badly: tears.

"Manuel? Manuel, can you hear me?"

Yes, I can, but I don't know how to let Julia know. I open my eyes, then quickly shut them. Next, I try to lift my arm, but it feels like it's strapped to the bed with steel bands. Thousands of ants crawl over me, piercing me with tiny holes and squirting acid under my skin.

I want to get away. Go back to my white room! But that's impossible. I've been thrown out of paradise into a hard, gray, burning reality.

"Manuel! Manuel!" Julia rests her hand on me. She doesn't know she's hurting me even more.

"We have to hurry!" Marten says. "That mercenary guy is close to breaking in!"

A muffled, distant banging punctuates his words. He puts one arm around my shoulders, the other under my knees, and lifts me up. It hurts like hell. I feel sick but there's nothing in my stomach to throw up.

He carries me up some steps and through a room that smells like chlorine. Smells! The fact that I have a sense of smell is the first piece of good news I've had since I woke up in this torture chamber of a body. I try opening my eyes again. It's less bright here so hurts less, but all I see are blurry shadows. Marten carries me past the swimming pool and into the basement corridor. The temperature drops. I can breathe without wanting to scream. Above me, I hear footsteps coming down the stairs. Someone pulls open a door.

"Quick, in here," Dr. Friese whispers.

It's dark. I think I see the gleam of a mirror—the room with the virtual reality headsets. A door closes quietly.

I hear Pieter, scarily close and very angry. "Friese! What's going on? Where's Henning?"

"They have the boy!" I hear the doctor say. "Raffay and the girl have him. They're in the garage!"

"Don't take me for a fool, Friese!"

"It's true! They went that way!"

"And Henning?"

"He's in the operating theater. They shot him."

"Why didn't you stay with him?"

"I wanted to tell you, and I wanted to call the police."

"No cops! Go back and look after him. I'll sort those bastards out. They can't have gone far." A metal door slams. Then a door opens.

"Quick! He's in the garage. You can get out through the main entrance upstairs. Be careful!" Friese whispers.

"What about you?" Marten asks.

"I'll stay here and try to hold him up."

"Come with us. He'll kill you if he finds out you lied to him!"

"He has no reason. Pieter may be ruthless but he's not stupid. He won't kill me unless there's something in it for him. Go!"

"Thanks!" Julia says. "I'll never forget this!"

"Thank me by getting away and putting Henning Jaspers behind bars!"

Marten carries me upstairs to the ground floor. By now I can make out more of my surroundings. Unclear and blurry, like I need a strong pair of glasses, but with my own eyes at least. The pain is becoming more bearable too.

Julia opens the door and peers out. They wait.

"Where is he?" Marten asks.

"I don't know," Julia says. "I don't see him."

"Come on. We have to risk it. We'll just head for the gate and—"

"Damn!" Julia shouts, and slams the door shut. "He's seen us!

Oh God, he's seen us!" The next moment there's a bang as a bullet from Pieter's gun hits the door.

Julia carefully peers through the door's spyhole. "He's heading for the garage. What do we do now?"

"If we're lucky, Friese will have been smart enough to lock the garage door."

Seconds later, the sound of banging and swearing confirms our hope.

"Now what?" Julia says.

"He'll do one of two things. Either climb up to the first floor like he did before, or lie in wait until we come out. He knows Manuel needs urgent medical attention. Of course, there's a chance we might call the police and he won't be able to do anything once they're here. So he'll probably take the first option and go back into the house."

"Can't we just get him when he comes down the stairs?"

"I wouldn't underestimate him. He's a mercenary. Best we don't get into a gunfight. Quiet." The sound of glass shattering under the weight of heavy kicking comes from the first floor. Julia and Marten run out of the house and he closes the door behind him as quietly as possible.

I try to say something. "Ga . . . ga . . ."

"Manuel? Manuel, was that you?"

"Ga . . . garden," I splutter. It feels like I'm spewing out a piece of burning coal.

"What do you mean?" Julia asks.

"Shh!" Marten snaps. He sticks close to the house wall, past the outdoor pool and through thick bushes. There's a gunshot as we turn the corner of the building.

"Run!" Marten sprints as fast as he can while carrying me—he's wheezing by the time he reaches the end of the garden. The ladder they used to climb over the wall is around fifty yards away, on the other side of an exposed lawn. A proficient gunman like Pieter will have no problem hitting two people running, especially when one of them is carrying a badly wounded boy. There's only one hope.

"The car! Quick!" Marten yells.

Julia gets to the black SUV first, pulls open the side door, and jumps in. The engine is still running, just like I left it after I used it to attack Pieter. Marten throws me into the passenger seat next to Julia like I'm a sack of potatoes. Another shot rings out. Marten screams, runs around the car, and jumps behind the wheel. The left sleeve of his black coverall is torn, and blood's pouring out.

"You're hurt!" Julia shouts.

"It's just a graze," Marten says, putting the car into manual drive and stepping on the accelerator.

Another shot hits and the windshield shatters, but luckily no one is hurt. Marten drives through the bushes in the front garden and presses the remote control stored in the central panel. The gate slowly slides open.

"Give me the gun!" Julia yells.

"No," Marten says. "It's too—"

Another shot rings out and the bullet hits the passenger seat.

"Come on!"

Marten gives her the gun. Julia leans over me, holds the pistol right by my head, points it through the broken side window, and pulls the trigger. The blast shatters my eardrum.

Finally, the gate opens wide enough for the car to get through. We turn into the road and Julia sobs with relief. I want to do the same, but all I manage is a painful groan as we tear through the night streets.

"How are you?" Julia asks.

Every part of me hurts, like someone's worked me over with a pair of pliers. I feel weak and the whole world is spinning. All right, I want to say, but all that comes out is a retching sound.

"Where are we actually going?" Julia asks Marten.

"My place."

"Shouldn't we get him to hospital as soon as possible?"

"Too dangerous. Jaspers would have no problem sending Pieter or someone else to make sure Manuel can never testify."

"Wouldn't he get police protection?"

"We can't rely on that. Trust me. We're better off at my place. I'm prepared and—Damn! What do we have to do to shake him off?"

Marten thrashes the steering wheel back and forth and we veer from side to side.

"What's happening?" Julia asks.

"Pieter. He's in the Ferrari. Crap!" There's a loud hooting sound as we head straight toward an oncoming car. Marten pulls to the right at the last minute. A second later, the traffic light at the junction ahead turns red. He presses the horn and keeps going, narrowly missing a car that's coming from the right. I see the driver through the side window. She has long black hair and is wearing a white dress.

We leave Hamburg city center and reach the outskirts. A shot hits our car and it starts to veer and shudder wildly. Marten struggles to keep it on the road.

"Damn!" he shouts. "He's shooting at the tires. If he hits the gas tank . . ."

I feel like a robot that's got no power. I gather all my strength, lean forward, and reach out my arm.

"Manuel!" Julia yells. "What are you doing? What are you up to?"

"Hesset!" I point at the virtual reality headset plugged into the central panel.

"You want to put on the headset. Why?"

"Hesset!" I repeat.

Julia gives me the headset. I put it on and press a switch. I see a virtual control panel. I can operate it using hand movements. Unfortunately, none of the programmers thought about the fact that it's hard to make hand movements when you're veering down the road in a speeding car and your arms feel like they weigh a hundred pounds. It takes me forever to complete the commands.

"What are you doing?" Julia asks.

I ignore her question and try to focus while Marten tries to stop Pieter from overtaking, but he just keeps shooting at us.

Finally, I manage to activate the drone that's in the back of the car. Got it! I see the picture from the drone's camera in the glasses and steer it through the car roof. It's pushed straight back by the air current. But instead of fighting against it, I use the wind's momentum and rev the drone harder. Pieter's eyes open wide. Then the drone smashes into the Ferrari's windshield and the picture turns black.

Marten cheers. "Yes! He's come off the road! You got him, Manuel!"

Julia takes the glasses off my face and kisses my cheek. "We're nearly there. Hold on, bro!"

I manage to stay conscious, and a little while later we head down a driveway and stop in front of a large stone house that looks like it used to be part of a farm.

Marten hoots the horn twice. The front door opens and a woman rushes out. Marten steps out of the car and opens the passenger door. The woman runs forward and lifts me out of the car like I'm a newborn baby. She has short blonde hair and warm eyes. She looks a bit like Eva, but is much older.

"Hello, Manuel!" she says. "I'm so glad you made it!"

She carries me into the house and up to the second floor, then lays me on a bed in a room with walls covered in Disney posters and shelves of toys. The room starts to spin. I try to hold on to reality, but it's like a dark eddy is dragging me down into oblivion.

CHAPTER 21

When I wake up, there's no pain. My mouth is dry and my head feels stuffed full of cotton. I don't recognize the room around me. Where am I? What happened?

Memories slowly come back: the escape from Jaspers's house, the car chase, and the kind woman who carried me into the house like I was a helpless baby. I feel a wave of relief—I'm safe!—but it's quickly replaced by doubt. Will Jaspers give up that easily? Will he send a hitman after me? Pieter, maybe? Oddly, I'm worried the South African may have been hurt in the car accident. Even though, given the order, he'd have no problem killing me.

I slowly sit up in bed, close my eyes for a second to stop the spinning, and then look around. The action figures, toy cars, and books on *Minecraft* tell me that the room belongs to a boy of around ten. I didn't know Marten had a son, but there's lots I don't know.

I remember what the doctor said: *He'll get his memory back as soon as the bioelectrical impulse inhibitors are deactivated.* But my head's still a blank. I try to remember what my room looked like, but all that comes up is the room Jaspers showed me—the fake room. Disappointment brings tears to my eyes. I don't even know whether I had my own room at my adoptive parents' house, or whether I shared with Julia.

Julia. She's the key to my past. I have to talk to her.

I carefully push myself to the edge of the bed and try to stand. The world spins. I wait for the room to stop moving, get up slowly, and stagger a few steps to the door, which has a blue terry-cloth dressing gown hanging from a hook. All I'm wearing is pajamas, so I grab the dressing gown. It's much too small but will do.

The door leads into a corridor with wooden floors and stone walls. Dark beams support the ceiling. The sound of voices comes through a half-open door on the ground floor and I manage to get downstairs by gripping on to the banister and taking one careful step after another.

I walk into a cozy kitchen. Marten, Julia, the woman from last night (who I guess is Marten's wife), and a man with gray hair wearing a suit and tie, sit at a large table covered in breakfast dishes. They're shocked to see me.

"Manuel!" The woman jumps up and holds me by the arm. "Why . . . you shouldn't be up! You're much too weak." She sounds concerned rather than annoyed. She walks me to a chair and I sit down gratefully. "I'm Gisa, Marten's wife," she says. "And this is Dr. Kerber, our lawyer." The man in the suit nods at me.

"How are you?" Julia asks, looking worried.

"Good," I say. My mouth feels like sandpaper and it's hard to speak, so I leave it at that.

Gisa puts a glass of lukewarm tap water in front of me. "Here, drink this."

I'm happy to do as she says, but the water makes me nauseous and I feel dizzy again.

"You should lie down," Marten says. "You're not strong enough yet."

I intend to shake my head, but instead everything turns black.

I'm back in bed. Orange evening light streams through the window. That means I've been asleep all day. My head feels twice its normal size, as though a hundred angry dwarves are hammering inside my skull. My eyes burn. My mouth is completely dry, my tongue swollen. No way could I stand up.

Gisa arrives with a glass of water and a handful of pills. "Take these, they'll help."

I swallow them gratefully. A little while later, the dwarves put down their hammers and I sink into a deep, dreamless sleep.

I wake up to a boring pain across my whole body, especially my head, swallow pills, drink, sleep. I don't know how often I repeat the routine. At some point I wake up and realize there's an IV tube in my left arm. It leads to a bag of clear liquid that's hanging on a green stand. I tentatively touch my head, which was totally bald when I first escaped. A fine down has grown since then, at least on the bits that aren't covered in bandages.

When Gisa arrives with my pills, I turn them down. My head hurts like hell but I don't want to slip back into a semi-conscious state.

"Okay," she says simply, gives me the water glass, and leaves.

The dwarves hollowing out my head have stopped using manual tools and moved on to jackhammers. A million ants help them by gnawing through my skin and into my body. I grip my head to stop it from exploding.

Turning down the pills was a mistake. If only Gisa would come back, I'd beg her for the drugs. I don't have enough strength to call her.

Slowly, very slowly, the pain subsides. My head still pounds but it's bearable.

Gisa suddenly appears. "How are you?" she says.

I groan. It's the best I can do.

"Do you want some painkillers?"

"No . . . it's . . . it's all right," I grunt.

"Are you hungry?"

My stomach rumbles in answer to the question. "Yes."

"I'll make you soup." She disappears.

For the first time in what might be days—I can't tell how long I've been here—I take a look around. Even though I hurt like crazy, I'm happy.

Gisa comes back carrying a tray with a steaming bowl of

chicken soup, a chunk of bread, and a glass of milk. "Whose room is this?" I ask her.

A shadow falls across her face. "Tim's," she replies. "He was our son. He died a few years ago."

"Oh. I'm sorry. I . . ."

"It's all right. You couldn't have known."

I want to find out more about Tim but it seems wrong to ask, so I eat the soup in silence. It tastes really good and gives me a little energy.

"Thanks, that was really good," I say when she takes the tray.

After carrying the tray down to the kitchen, Gisa comes back and deftly removes the IV tube from my arm. "You don't need this anymore."

"How do . . . Where did you learn to do that?"

"I'm a trained nurse. Worked at the university clinic for ten years."

"Thanks," I say again. "To you and Marten for helping me."

"No need. We couldn't exactly leave you in the hands of a ruthless criminal." Her eyes flash with anger.

"Can I . . . speak to Julia, please?"

"She's with your adoptive parents."

I'm stunned. "But . . ."

"Don't worry. They're still your legal guardians, but Dr. Kerber, the lawyer, is making sure they lose their rights. In any case, you're safe here for now."

My stomach spasms at the thought of ending up with the

people who sold me off to Henning Jaspers. And I'm upset Julia isn't here. I'd hoped she would tell me about my life and help me get back my memory.

"Can I phone her?"

"We've arranged for her to call us regularly. I'll let you know next time she calls."

"What . . . what will happen to me now?"

"First, you need to get well. Marten and Dr. Kerber are working out a plan for how to deal with Jaspers. You're the star witness in a lawsuit that could take years." Her expression turns somber. "Henning is cunning. He'll use all the tricks in the book to get away with this. But we'll get him this time, I promise!"

"What do you mean, 'this time'?" I ask, but Gisa doesn't say.

"I have a couple of things to take care of and need to leave you for a bit. If you need anything, just yell." And with that, she leaves the room.

I lie there and try to remember something, anything, from my childhood. But there's nothing, it's as though my life began when I woke up in the white room.

My gaze falls on the shelves full of toys and children's books. Maybe Tim had something I might remember playing with? I carefully stand up. My legs feel like boiled spaghetti, so I crawl to the shelf on all fours. I pick up toys, touch and smell them: action figures, Lego models, a small microscope, a stuffed toy dog with huge, anxious eyes, a basketball. But none of it triggers anything.

There's a shelf full of books on *Minecraft*. There are lots of manga series too, all neatly lined up in numerical order, and a load of picture books. Among all these, I find a book with an old, yellowing spine that doesn't really seem to fit into this kid's room: *Alice's Adventures in Wonderland* by Lewis Carroll.

CHAPTER 22

My hands shake as I carefully pull the book off the shelf. The cover looks fragile. Underneath the gold-embossed, delicately bordered title, there's a drawing of a puzzled dog staring at a tiny Alice. *Leipzig Publishing, Johann Fr. Hartknoch.* I open the book carefully. The pages smell dusty and look like they'll fall apart if I turn them.

The publication date printed on the inside cover is 1869. Is this a first edition? It must be quite valuable! Why is such an expensive book on the shelf among all these tattered comic books?

"What are you doing?" Gisa's voice is sharp, like I've done something wrong.

I almost drop the book in surprise and turn around. "I . . . I thought . . . maybe I could . . ."

"You should stay in bed!" she says sternly. "You're much too weak to be up!" She takes the book and puts it back on the shelf.

I obediently crawl back into bed. "The book . . . did it belong to your son?"

"Yes. It was his favorite story. Marten always used to read it to him, especially when . . ." She falters, unable to say more.

"I'm sorry." I seem to have stirred up bad memories.

"Don't worry. Just don't touch his things, okay?"

"Yes, of course."

"Best you sleep for a bit," she says in a gentler tone, leaving the room.

But I'm not tired. My gaze keeps drifting back to the shelf. I don't know why but I'm totally drawn to the book. It must mean something to me.

I wrestle with myself for a bit. I don't want to hurt Gisa and Marten's feelings. It must be painful to them that I'm here in their dead son's room: a room they may not have gone into for a long time. On the other hand, I need my memory back and the book could help.

In the end, my curiosity wins. I stand up gingerly, stagger to the shelf on wobbly legs, take the book, and quickly lie back down. My heart's pounding as I open the book and start reading:

Chapter One
Down the Rabbit-Hole

Alice was beginning to get very tired of sitting by her sister on the bank, and of having nothing to do: once or twice she had peeped into the book her sister was reading, but it had no pictures or conversations in it, 'and what is the use of a book,' thought Alice 'without pictures or conversations?'

So she was considering in her own mind (as well as she could, for the hot day made her feel very sleepy and stupid), whether the pleasure of making a daisy-chain would be worth the trouble of getting up and picking the daisies, when suddenly a White Rabbit with pink eyes ran close by her.

There was nothing so *very* remarkable in that; nor did Alice think it so *very* much out of the way to hear the Rabbit say to itself, 'Oh dear! Oh dear! I shall be late!' (when she thought it over afterwards, it occurred to her that she ought to have wondered at this, but at the time it all seemed quite natural); but when the Rabbit actually *took a watch out of its waistcoat-pocket*, and looked at it, and then hurried on, Alice started to her feet, for it flashed across her mind that she had never before seen a rabbit with either a waistcoat-pocket, or a watch to take out of it, and burning with curiosity, she ran across the field after it, and fortunately was just in time to see it pop down a large rabbit-hole under the hedge.

In another moment down went Alice after it, never once considering how in the world she was to get out again.

The rabbit-hole went straight on like a tunnel

for some way, and then dipped suddenly down, so suddenly that Alice had not a moment to think about stopping herself before she found herself falling down a very deep well.

I'm overcome with dizziness and feel like I'm the one falling down a well. I put down the book and stare at the ceiling until the feeling passes, then go back to reading.

Either the well was very deep, or she fell very slowly, for she had plenty of time as she went down to look about her and to wonder what was going to happen next. First, she tried to look down and make out what she was coming to, but it was too dark to see anything; then she looked at the sides of the well, and noticed that they were filled with cupboards and book-shelves; here and there she saw maps and pictures hung upon pegs. She took down a jar from one of the shelves as she passed; it was labelled 'ORANGE MARMALADE', but to her great disap-pointment it was empty: she did not like to drop the jar for fear of killing somebody underneath, so man-aged to put it into one of the cupboards as she fell past it.

'Well!' thought Alice to herself, 'after such a fall as this, I shall think nothing of tumbling down stairs! How brave they'll all think me at home! Why, I wouldn't say anything about it, even if I fell off the top of the house!' (Which was very likely true.)

Down, down, down. Would the fall *never* come to an end? 'I wonder how many miles I've fallen by this time?' she said aloud. 'I must be getting somewhere near the centre of the earth. Let me see: that would be eight hundred and fifty miles down, I think—'

Someone's scribbled a note in the margin here: *Not true*. Did Tim write this, or was it someone who owned the book before him? In actual fact, the Earth's radius does measure way more than 850 miles. But how do I know that? Did I learn it in a geography lesson? Or did I read it somewhere?

I turn back to the story. It feels familiar. I'm sure I've read this story often, or maybe someone used to read it to me. But I can't picture a face, a voice, or a room I might have held the book in.

. . . she found herself in a long, low hall, which was lit up by a row of lamps hanging from the roof.

There were doors all round the hall, but they were all locked; and when Alice had been all the way down one side and up the other, trying every door, she walked sadly down the middle, wondering how she was ever to get out again.

This section reminds me of the white room, my confusion, the feeling that I would never escape that prison. My body starts to shake at the memory and my eyes fill with tears. A drop lands on the book and I quickly wipe it away before it damages the aging paper.

I hear footsteps outside the door and slip the book under the covers. Marten comes in.

"Hello, Manuel. How are you?"

"Better, thanks."

He looks at me closely. "Have you been crying?"

"I . . . I still can't remember stuff."

"Don't worry, I'm sure you'll get your memory back soon. Your brain was badly injured, but I'm sure it will heal."

"I really want to talk to Julia. It might help if she could tell me things about my past."

He nods. "Yes, of course that would help. She's in foster care at the moment. Let me see if I can get ahold of her."

I frown. "Gisa said she was with our adoptive parents."

"Er, she was, but she didn't want to stay there. We asked social services to collect her and take her somewhere safe."

"Why . . . why can't she come here?"

He hesitates. "On legal grounds. It's a little complicated, but Dr. Kerber thinks it's best if you're not here together. It's something to do with your credibility as witnesses."

"I don't understand."

"I can't explain it better than that, but Dr. Kerber is a good lawyer so best we do as he says if we're going to fight Henning. Don't worry. I'll call her so you can talk. I'll be right back."

He leaves the room and comes back a few minutes later. "I couldn't reach her. I left a message on her voice mail. I'll let you know as soon as she phones back."

I look at him for a second. Why do I suddenly feel he's holding back?

"Tell me about Tim," I say.

His face darkens and I expect a curt reply, but he pulls over the desk chair and sits next to the bed.

"He was . . . an amazing kid, smart, gentle, curious." Marten's eyes fill with tears and I feel bad for doubting him. "He was ten when he died. He'd be around your age now."

"How did he die?"

"He had a genetic condition, a rare form of muscle weakness that deteriorates quickly and is incurable. We . . . we did everything we could to help him . . . but . . . ." He can't go on.

"I'm really sorry."

"That's okay. Sorry, I . . . I should be over it by now, but . . ." I don't want to cause Marten any more pain, but he keeps talking. "We were both so proud of him, Gisa and I. He was really good in school, wanted to become a games programmer, like me. He spent a lot of time on the computer, even taught himself programming. Actually, I wasn't too happy about that, but—"

"Did he like reading too?" I blurt out.

"You mean books? Yes, he did. I would often read to him. His favorite book was *Alice's Adventures in Wonderland*." He gets up and goes to the shelf. "I bought him a valuable first edition for his birthday. It's here somewhere . . ."

I feel myself turn red as I finger the book hidden under the covers. Luckily he doesn't notice. I don't know why I don't just say I have it—I guess I feel bad because Gisa asked me not to touch anything.

"Hmm," Marten says. "Maybe Gisa moved it. It doesn't matter. So now you know why we used imagery from that book. Julia told me you used to love the book when you were a kid and I thought it was pretty much a sign from the universe."

I suddenly feel shabby, like an intruder, an unwanted guest. I'm lying in Gisa and Marten's son's bed, a boy who died in pain. I may have my own problems but at least I'm not terminally ill.

"Thanks for helping me," I say.

"That's all right, son. I would never have forgiven myself if you'd gone through the same thing . . . if you'd died at Henning's hands."

I'm struck by a thought. "When did you argue with Henning Jaspers?"

"Around five years ago. Why?"

"Was it anything to do with Tim's death?"

He looks away. "No, of course not. At least, not directly. I was under a lot of pressure at the time, as you can imagine. And when Henning started to go off on his immortality trip just when my son was on his deathbed, I lost it. I accused him of a load of stuff, and he took it badly. It doesn't matter . . ." He checks his watch. "I need to call Dr. Kerber. Feel better, Manuel."

"Thanks."

His abrupt response and the way he hurries out of the room confirm my suspicion: Marten is lying. It can't be a coincidence that he fell out with Henning exactly at the time Tim died. Was the whole idea of extending life through a virtual world actually Marten's idea, not Jaspers's? Was it his way of trying to save his son? But why would he be so secretive and lie?

Maybe he feels responsible for what happened to me, I think, answering my own question. Or . . .

I come up with a theory: If it really was Marten's idea, maybe they worked together to find a way to keep a brain alive inside a virtual world—Tim's only hope. But they weren't fast enough and Tim died before the computer–brain interface and life support machines were ready. Marten wanted to stop the project, but Jaspers wanted to keep going, hoping to extend his own life one day. They fought. Jaspers squeezed Marten out of the company. Marten found out Jaspers was performing illegal experiments in order to test the computer–brain interface and decided to report him to the authorities.

Is that the only reason he helped me escape Jaspers? For revenge? Did he just use Julia as bait? Am I nothing more than a trial witness? A tool for bringing down his former business partner? I want to get up and ask, but I'm too weak.

The book is pressed against my leg. I take it out to put it

away but then I'm struck by a thought: Maybe Tim wrote more notes in the margin that could give me clues as to what happened to him.

I flick through the pages and in Chapter Five come across passages underlined in blue ink:

Chapter Five
Advice from a Caterpillar

The Caterpillar and Alice looked at each other for some time in silence: at last the Caterpillar took the hookah out of its mouth, and addressed her in a languid, sleepy voice.

'Who are you?' said the Caterpillar.

This was not an encouraging opening for a conversation. Alice replied, rather shyly, <u>'I—I hardly know, sir, just at present—at least I know who I</u> was <u>when I got up this morning, but I think I must have been changed several times since then.'</u>

'What do you mean by that?' said the Caterpillar sternly. 'Explain yourself!'

'I can't explain myself, I'm afraid, sir,' said Alice, 'because I'm not myself, you see.'

'I don't see,' said the Caterpillar

'I'm afraid I can't put it more clearly,' Alice replied very politely, <u>'for I can't understand it myself</u> to begin

with; and being so many different sizes in a day is very confusing.'

A chill runs down my spine as I read the passage over and over. Yes, that's exactly how I feel—like I'm not *me*. Why did Tim underline exactly these passages? Did he feel the same? But he was at home, safe, with his parents, memory intact. But then, it might not have been Tim who underlined the passages . . .

A terrible thought crosses my mind. I carefully stand up and stagger to Tim's desk. I find a notepad and pen in one of the drawers. I scribble *Not true* on the page and hold it against the open book. There's no doubt: It's the same handwriting—I wrote the note in the margin.

Am I Tim?

CHAPTER 23

"Manuel!" Gisa snaps. "What are you doing? You shouldn't be up!"

I flinch, and turn slowly. My eyes are brimming with tears that cloud the partly concerned, partly annoyed look on Gisa's face. "Who . . . who am I?"

"What do you mean?"

"This is my handwriting." I point, first at the notepad, then at the scribbles in the book.

"How could you?" Gisa says, outraged. "That was Tim's favorite book! Do you have any idea how much that cost? I told you not to touch his things!"

Her reaction throws me. "The note was there when I took the book off the shelf. So I would need to have written it before I was even with Henning Jaspers. Please, Gisa, what's going on?"

She pins me with an appraising glare and rests a hand on my forehead. "Hmm. You don't have a fever, but you're clearly having memory lapses."

"What do you mean?"

"Manuel, that book belonged to Tim." She sounds concerned. "I don't know why you scribbled in it, but you seem to have forgotten you did. We may need to call a neurologist after all. There seems to be more brain damage than we'd thought."

I stare at the book. Again, I have an awful feeling that I'm not me. Did I really read the book, make notes in the margins, underline sentences, and then forget I'd done anything?

Her voice is gentle but firm, like she's talking to a young child. "Manuel, you're still very weak. You should rest."

"I have to speak to Julia," I beg. "Please!"

"I said I would put you on just as soon as she calls. Have a nap, I'm sure you'll feel better." She helps me hobble back to bed. Then she puts the book back on the shelf.

Dazed, I watch her leave the room, then I lie there for a long time trying to make sense of what just happened. But my pointless thoughts spin around like a cat chasing its tail. In the end, exhaustion gets the better of me and I fall asleep.

I wander through a forest. It's not a real forest, but a roughly drawn cartoon forest with black tree trunks and bare branches that seem to be reaching out to grab me. Everything is unfamiliar and strange, but I feel like I've been here before.

"So, who do we have here?" someone says.

I turn and see a cartoon cat with an unfeasibly wide grin, sitting on a branch. Its fur is pink with purple pajama-like stripes.

"Where . . . where am I?" I ask.

"Where would you like to be?" the grinning cat answers.

"In the real world," I say after thinking about it for a second.

"In that case you've taken a wrong turn."

I try to remember what happens in the book. I think the Cheshire Cat tells Alice how to find the Mad Hatter, but I'm not sure how he can help me.

"Am I dreaming?" I say.

"Well, that depends," the cat replies.

"On what?"

"On whether you're asleep."

Very helpful. "Could you tell me how to wake up?"

"Of course." The cat gives a wide yawn, showing off its very sharp teeth—now it looks like a cat in a computer game.

"How?"

"Open your eyes!"

I open my eyes and look around, startled. It's dark, just like in the cartoon forest. Then, in the pale moonlight, I make out the shapes of Tim's room: the wardrobe near the door, the shelves with toys and books, the desk, the posters on the walls. I sigh, relieved.

The dream replays in my mind. It was so real, like I actually was in Wonderland. *Open your eyes*, the cat said. I'm struck by something: How can I be sure my eyes are open? That I'm not just dreaming? I touch my eyelashes, the glassy surface of my right eyeball under the eyelid. But what's the point? That could just be part of a dream too.

I try to sleep but can't. Hundreds of questions keep me awake: Why hasn't my memory come back yet? How did my handwriting get in Tim's book? And most of all, where is Julia? Why hasn't she been in touch?

The longer I lie there brooding, the more sure I am that Gisa and Marten are keeping us apart. I don't know why, but they're lying to me. Just like Jaspers, they don't want me to find out the truth. They're probably using me to get back at him. And used Julia to gain my trust and get to me. Now they don't need her anymore so are keeping her away.

What if they hurt her? The thought hits a nerve. Julia and I are orphans. Jaspers paid off our adoptive parents and they probably won't even care we're gone or report us missing. Probably, no one would notice if Julia disappeared. But that's ridiculous. There's not even the tiniest shred of evidence for my unlikely theory. Still, I can't bear lying in bed doing nothing. I feel cut off from the world, almost like I'm back in the white room.

Clouds drift across the moonlit sky and Tim's room fills with light and then shadow. It feels more and more like a prison cell. I have to get out. If Julia can't come to me, I'll just have to go to her. I will find her, somehow. This time I won't have help, but at least I'm not hooked up to any machines, and there's no Pieter with a gun trying to stop me from getting away.

Outside, day is breaking. I get up and listen at the door. Everything's quiet. I push down the handle as silently as I can, but the door won't open. I've been locked in.

If I needed any more proof that Marten and Gisa plan to keep me here against my will, this is it. I hobble over to the window and look out. There's a swing and a sandbox that's overgrown with weeds in a small garden with fruit trees. Beyond a row of bushes, there's a field with cows, asleep on their feet. Behind that I see a road with streetlights. Not many cars will be going past at this time of day. I'm on the first floor but could climb down using bed-sheets. And then what? No idea. The main thing is to get away. I'll think of something once I finally have control of my own life.

The window has a rotary handle with a small keyhole. It won't budge. I vainly tug at it. Should I break the glass? No—the noise would wake Gisa and Marten.

I search the room for something to use as a tool to pry open the lock, but can't find anything. I head back over to window and look out, defeated. And then I shudder.

A woman is standing in the field among the sleeping cows. Her snow-white dress glows in the moonlight.

CHAPTER 24

The woman in white looks at me. Even though she's at least a hundred yards away, her gentle gaze seems familiar.

I blink, rub my eyes, shake my head, but the apparition doesn't disappear. I lift an arm and wave, but she doesn't react.

A thought crosses my mind: Maybe she's a ghost. My dead mother, who keeps showing up to help and encourage me—or something. As far as I know, I've never believed in life after death. But what I believe makes no difference to anything.

I decide to photograph the woman. If, as I suspect, she's just a hallucination, then she won't show on the picture. I search Tim's shelves for a cell phone or a kid's digital camera but find nothing. When I get back to the window, the apparition is gone. I'm relieved. And sad.

At least now there's no doubt that my brain's been badly injured. And no wonder, considering how much Jaspers and the doctor messed around with it. I should really be in hospital, maybe even in a psychiatric unit. Either way, Gisa is right, and probably locked me in for my own safety. Even so, I feel uneasy.

Around an hour later, I hear the key turn in the lock. Gisa comes in carrying a breakfast tray with a jug of milk, two slices of toast with jam, and a soft-boiled egg.

"Why did you lock the door?" I ask.

"So you wouldn't fall down the stairs again," she says, putting the tray on the bed.

"Again? What do you mean?"

"Last week, you had a bad fall. Don't you remember?"

"No," I say, unnerved.

She looks at me, worried, but says nothing. "Eat your breakfast, Timmy. You need to rebuild your strength."

I stare at her. "Timmy?"

"What?"

"You just called me Timmy!"

"Did I? Sorry."

"What about Julia? Do I get to speak to her today?"

"Yes, definitely. I'll try her later." She almost sounds annoyed. "Eat. I'll come back for the tray in a bit." And with that, she leaves the room.

Once I've had breakfast, I go to the bathroom to the left of Tim's room. I look in the mirror and I'm shocked. The face staring back at me doesn't look like my face. I touch my cheek and the young man mirrors my action, but he still doesn't feel like me.

The words underlined in the book run through my head: *I know who I was when I got up this morning, but I think I must have been changed several times since then.*

My reflection fogs with tears. Somehow that makes it look more familiar.

After washing my face and brushing my teeth with a brand-new toothbrush, I go back to Tim's room. Gisa has cleared the tray while I've been gone. Without hesitating, I take the old book from the shelf, sit on the bed, and flick through the yellowing pages. A black-and-white drawing jumps out at me: the Cheshire Cat, sitting in a tree, looking down at Alice. A chill runs down my spine when I remember my scarily real dream. I read:

The Cat only grinned when it saw Alice. It looked good-natured, she thought: still it had very *long claws and a great many teeth, so she felt that it ought to be treated with respect.*

'Cheshire Puss,' she began, rather timidly, as she did not at all know whether it would like the name: however, it only grinned a little wider. 'Come, it's pleased so far,' thought Alice, and she went on. 'Would you tell me, please, which way I ought to go from here?'

'That depends a good deal on where you want to get to,' said the Cat.

'I don't much care where—' said Alice after think-ing it over for a moment.

'In that case you've taken a wrong turn,' explained the Cat.

Alice found the answer rather bewildering.

'Am I dreaming?' she asked.

'Well, that depends,' the Cat replied.

'On what?' Alice asked.

'On whether you're asleep,' the Cat replied.

Again, this did not seem terribly helpful. 'Please, dear Cheshire Cat, could you tell me how to wake up?'

'Of course,' said the Cat, giving a yawn and open-ing its very large mouth wide so that Alice could see its sharp teeth. At that moment, the Cat looked rather like a terrible monster out of the Chamber of Horrors at the Annual Fair.

Although she was a little afraid, Alice bravely asked: 'So what do you advise, noble Cat?'

'Open your eyes!' the Cat replied.

I read the section over and over. The conversation between Alice and the Cheshire Cat is exactly like the one in the dream I had right before I woke up. I've read the book so often before and probably know bits by heart, so that's easy enough to explain. But why does the passage seem so odd, so wrong?

I keep reading:

Alice really did try to follow the cat's advice, but this proved to be terribly difficult as her eyes were already open. She realized it was an impossible task; and that she would just have to keep on dreaming, if this really was a dream. So she tried another question. 'What sort of people live about here?'

'In that direction,' the Cat said, waving its right paw round, 'lives a Hatter: and in that direction,' waving the other paw, 'lives a March Hare. Visit either you like: they're both mad.'

'But I don't want to go among mad people,' Alice remarked.

'Oh, you can't help that,' said the Cat: "we're all mad here. I'm mad. You're mad.'

'How do you know I'm mad?' said Alice.

'You must be,' said the Cat, 'or you wouldn't have come here.'

It's as though the Cheshire Cat is talking right at me: *You're mad, Manuel. You must be, or you wouldn't be here . . .*

Where am I? I look around the child's room. Is what I'm looking at real, or just some weird dream? *Open your eyes!* I wish I could.

The book feels heavy in my hands. Suddenly I'm scared of getting even more lost. I want to slam the book shut, but it keeps drawing me in.

So I keep reading about how Alice meets the Mad Hatter at the Tea Party. The story seems strangely twisted and confused, with no clear storyline or inner logic, as though Lewis Carroll never planned a plot but just wrote down whatever was going on in his head. Was this confused mess really one of my favorite books? Did Tim actually like it?

Before long, I lose interest and flick through the pages until I come across another note, scribbled in the margins by someone— me? That section of the book reads:

> *'I could tell you my adventures—beginning from this morning,' said Alice a little timidly: 'but it's no use going back to yesterday, because I was a different person then.'*
>
> *'Explain all that,' said the Mock Turtle.*

'No, no! The adventures first,' said the Gryphon in an impatient tone: 'explanations take such a dreadful time.'

> *So Alice began telling them her adventures from the time she first reached the white room. She was a little nervous about it just at first, the two creatures got so close to her, one on each side, and opened their eyes and mouths so very wide, but she gained courage as she went on. Her listeners were perfectly quiet till*

she got to the part about her repeating 'You are old, Father William,' *to the Caterpillar, and the words all coming different, and then the Mock Turtle drew a long breath, and said, 'That's very curious.'*

'It's all about as curious as it can be,' said the Gryphon.

I stop short. My eyes scan back up a few lines. That is actually what it says: *So Alice began telling them her adventures from the time she first reached the white room.* I read the line over and over. Even though I don't remember the last time I read *Alice's Adventures in Wonderland*, I'm pretty sure there was no mention of a white room.

CHAPTER 25

My fingers tremble as I flick forward a few pages, then back, but the words don't change: Instead of *white rabbit*, it clearly says *white room*.

I'm freaking out and toss the book across the room like it's a bomb. It slams against the bookshelf. Just then, Gisa and Marten come in. I flinch, expecting them to scold me for mishandling a valuable book. But they say nothing—either they didn't notice or decide to ignore it.

"Manuel, we need to talk," Gisa says.

"We have a proposition," Marten continues. He sits on the edge of the bed and Gisa settles into the office chair next to Tim's desk. They look at me, deadly serious.

"We . . . we were wondering . . ." Marten begins, ". . . whether you . . . of course, only if you agree . . ."

"We wanted to ask if you would be our son, Manuel," Gisa ends his broken sentence.

I look at them in amazement. "You . . . you want to adopt me?"

"It would make things a lot easier," Gisa explains. "That way, we could represent you when we take Jaspers to court and sue for damages. Child services have already said they'd approve."

"We know we could never replace your biological parents," Marten says. "But we'd try to treat you like ... like you were our son."

"What about Julia?" I say. "Would you adopt her too?"

"That's not possible, I'm afraid," Gisa replies.

"Why not?"

"Social services would never approve a double adoption," Marten says.

That seems ridiculous. "But she's my sister!"

"Not exactly," Gisa replies. "You grew up together, that's true. But she's not your biological sister."

"What? But ... but Julia said—"

"Julia doesn't know," Marten explains. "Dr. Kerber only just found out. He checked the adoption papers. You're not actually related. Your adoptive parents took you both from the orphanage because you had such a close bond that even the carers thought you were brother and sister. That's why social services made an exception and agreed to a double adoption back then. But things are different now; you're old enough to go your separate ways."

"You're lying!" I shout. "You just want to use me to get Jaspers. You used Julia and now you don't need her anymore so want to keep us apart! She's my sister, I just know it!"

"Calm down, Timmy," Gisa says. "You don't have a sister."

I can't speak straightaway and just stare at them, full of hate. "I-I'm not Timmy!" I say in the end.

Gisa laughs. "You'll always be our Timmy!"

What's going on? What the hell is going on? Has Gisa totally lost her mind? Or have I? For a second, I'm not even sure whether I am actually Tim or Manuel. Then I remember the white room and all the lies, and realize nothing they've told me is true.

I get up even though my body is tired and heavy.

"Where are you going, Timmy?" Gisa asks. "You're too weak to be up."

"I need the bathroom," I say. They don't stop me from leaving.

"He needs some time," I hear Marten say. "He's not ready."

Once I'm in the corridor, I quickly shut the bedroom door and turn the key. Now *they're* locked in!

"Hey, what's going on?" Marten yells. "Open the door right now!"

"Timmy!" I hear Gisa shout. "Timmy, my God! Come back, son!"

I have to get out of this madhouse! I hurry downstairs, steadying myself on the banister. While Gisa and Marten hammer the bedroom door shouting "Timmy!," I run for the front door. All I'm wearing is a dressing gown, so I grab a padded raincoat that's hanging near the entrance. But the door won't open.

Damn! They probably thought I'd make a run for it and locked the door just in case. I quickly look around. A few doors lead off the hall into adjoining rooms: the kitchen, where I sat with them, Julia, and the lawyer; a small pantry; a guest toilet; and a big living room with a glass door that leads onto the garden. That's my way out!

But just as I'm heading there, I notice a door under the stairs that probably leads to the basement. It has an electronic lock and there's a small keypad on the door frame.

I freeze, staring at the gap between the door and the floor. A bright white light shines through. As though someone is shining headlights through the crack. I want to run, but my legs won't move.

A loud thud pulls me out of my trance. They've broken down the door!

"Timmy!" Gisa yells, hurrying downstairs. "Wait!"

I run into the living room. The door to the garden is locked too.

I desperately look around, grab a big blue-painted vase off the coffee table, and fling it against the door. The vase breaks. The glass door shatters, forming a web of cracks, but it doesn't break. I wrap the raincoat around my right hand and punch bits of glass away from the frame, but before I can make a hole big enough to get through, Gisa and Marten burst into the room. Marten grabs me and pulls me back.

"My God, son, you're going to hurt yourself!" he yells.

"Hold on to him!" Gisa says.

I struggle, confused, but I'm too weak to escape Marten's iron grip. "Let go!" I shout. "I want to see Julia! I want Julia!"

From nowhere, Gisa is holding a syringe. I feel a quick stab in my thigh. Seconds later, a warm, soft blanket of darkness falls over me.

My last thought is: *Jaspers was right.* I shouldn't have trusted Marten.

CHAPTER 26

'm wandering through a cartoon forest, back in the dream where I met the Cheshire Cat. I reach a clearing. There's a crooked house with a thatched roof and two chimney stacks in the shape of rabbit ears. Three cartoon characters sit at a long table set for a meal: a rabbit with lopsided ears and bulging eyes, a guy with a hat that's too big, and a dozing furry creature that must be a dormouse.

"What are you doing here?" the rabbit says. "There's no space!"

"There's nothing for you here!" the Mad Hatter says.

I can think of many places I'd rather be than in this dream, which feels just as unsettlingly real as it did last time. I look around: I have a cartoon body dressed in pajamas. Even so, I pinch myself just to check, and feel pain in the backs of my hands. The stuff Gisa gave me must have been pretty strong.

I wait for a while, undecided, hoping something will happen— if I'm not going to wake up, then at least I could change dreams.

Instead, I just stand there while the rabbit and Mad Hatter slurp their tea.

I really don't feel like joining the crazy cartoon figures, so I follow a winding path into the woods. After walking through the gloomy cartoon forest for a while, I reach a clearing with a thatched-roof house with rabbit ears and a long table outside.

"And you're back!" the rabbit complains. "Can't you see you don't belong here?"

"I would go so far as to suggest you've completely lost your way!" the Mad Hatter agrees.

"Leave me alone," I say, and take another path. But, of course, it brings me right back to where I started. I resign myself to sitting at the table.

"Hey, there's no space here!" the rabbit grumbles.

"All taken!" the Mad Hatter says.

"Shut your trap!" I reply.

"A little white wine, perhaps?" the rabbit asks.

"No thanks."

"Sorry, but I can't give you any white wine," the rabbit explains. "There's none left."

I ignore his rambling. "Where is Alice?" I ask.

"Alice who?" the rabbit says.

"I don't know an Alice," the Mad Hatter adds. "Never heard of her. Never will, as far as I can tell."

Just then, she walks out of the forest: a cartoon girl in a blue dress with a white pinafore. But her hair isn't blonde, it's black, and, even for a cartoon, she has really big, manga-character eyes.

"Julia!" I shout.

"Manuel!" she says. "At last!"

I start to cry.

"Hey, watch out!" the rabbit complains. "You're wetting the tablecloth!"

"May I join you?" cartoon Julia asks.

"Absolutely not!" the Mad Hatter says.

"There's no more space!" the rabbit agrees.

I've had enough! I lunge forward and push the table over. Teapots and crockery crash to the floor. "Enough!" I yell. "I've had enough of this dream! I want to wake up!"

"Young man, your behavior is appalling," the Mad Hatter grumbles, still sitting in his chair.

"And you've woken the dormouse!" the rabbit whines.

"What? Is it Thursday already?" the dormouse says, but is fast asleep two seconds later.

"Calm down, Manuel," Julia says. "It'll be all right!"

"The hell it will!" I shout. "Gisa and Marten have given me drugs. They want me to replace Timmy. They're keeping you away from me. Damn it, even though I know I'm dreaming I'm still talking to you as though you're here. What's wrong with me?"

Fat tears spurt out of my cartoon eyes as though they're squirting out of a fire hose. They fill the clearing, forming a big lake.

"I *am* here!" Julia says.

"Don't believe her!" the Mad Hatter declares. "It's just a dream!"

"But what if it isn't?" the rabbit asks.

What if it isn't? The thought gives me a jolt. My flood of tears dries up and I look around. This definitely isn't real. But if it's not a dream, then what is it?

"Am I in a simulation?" I say out loud. "Like Middle-earth?"

"Middle-earth?" the rabbit says. "I've never heard such nonsense! Middle-earth would have to lie between Lower Earth and Upper Earth. But it doesn't; I know what I'm talking about!"

I ignore his drivel. "Are you an NPC?" I ask Julia. "Or are we both trapped in a virtual world?"

"Finish the story!" she answers. "Find the code!"

What code? I'm about to ask—but then I remember.

"Cogito, ergo sum!" I shout, and open my eyes.

I'm back in Tim's bed. My head hurts as badly as it did when I escaped from Jaspers's house. I sit up and the room starts to spin. I feel sick. Probably a side effect from the drugs Gisa gave me.

I struggle against the dizziness and nausea. They can drug me all they want, but I won't give up that easily. I stagger to the door on shaking legs. Locked. There's no evidence that the door was smashed open recently. I pound the door feebly but either no one hears or they're just ignoring me.

"Let me out!" I yell, sounding like a slurring drunk. I feel like crying but my exhausted body can't even muster a sob.

The door opens. "Timmy!" Gisa says. "What are you doing? Marten, help!"

They heave me back onto the bed. I let them; don't even have the strength to defend myself.

Gisa leans over me. "Timmy!" she says. "My poor, poor boy." She kisses my forehead. I want to wipe away the wet patch left by her lips, but my arm is a dead weight. I close my eyes and wish myself away.

When I wake up, it's dark outside. My head still hurts but I feel less groggy. I lie there for a while trying to sort out my thoughts. Of everything that's happened, what's real and what's a dream? Did I really see a bright light streaming out from under the basement door? Did I throw a vase into the glass door in the living room or was that a dream? Wonderland was definitely a dream—or was it?

What if it's not?

I get up a while later and shuffle to the window. The moon is nearly full and illuminates the field with the cows. The woman in the white dress isn't there.

I turn on the light, take the book off the shelf, and turn the pages until I find the bit where Alice tells the Gryphon and Mock Turtle about her adventures. It's still there, the sentence that shouldn't be there, that can't be there: *So Alice began telling them her adventures from the time she first reached the white room.* I read the sentence over and over, touch the book, smell it, look at the stains on its cover that seem to prove without doubt that this book is over a hundred years old. What the hell does it all mean?

Then I remember what cartoon-Julia told me: *Finish the story. Find the code.*

I thought I knew the code.

What if I don't?

What if Wonderland is real and this is the dream? No, that's ridiculous. Yet there's something very wrong about the reality I think I'm in. Is it possible to tamper with an old book and add words Lewis Carroll definitely didn't write? But what would be the point? And why does Gisa keep calling me "Timmy"? Is she mad, or am *I*?

Finish the story.

I turn to the back of the book and read:

'Hold your tongue!' said the Queen, turning purple.

'I won't!' said Alice.

'Off with her head!' the Queen shouted at the top of her voice. Nobody moved.

'Who cares for you?' said Alice, (she had grown to her full size by this time.) 'You're nothing but a pack of cards!'

At this the whole pack rose up into the air, and came flying down upon her: she gave a little scream, half of fright and half of anger, and tried to beat them off, and found herself lying on the bank, with her

head in the lap of her sister, who was gently brushing
away some dead leaves that had fluttered down from
the trees upon her face.

I look around Tim's room. Is this real, or a dream? How can I ever be sure?

Finish the story.

I read the final paragraphs and close the book. Nothing has changed. I open the book and find the sentence about the white room, and the note in my handwriting that's all the way at the beginning: *Not true.* The book is trying to tell me something. But what?

I read the bit right before Alice wakes up: *You're nothing but a pack of cards!* Nothing more than a game . . . is that what it means? Is this a sick game someone's playing with me? But who, and why?

I have an idea. I look through Tim's toys and find a worn deck of cards inside a box. When I examine them, I realize that the picture cards have the wrong letter in the corner: the King of Hearts has an *M* instead of a *K*; the Queen of Hearts has an *E* instead of a *Q*. I quickly dig out the other face cards and lay them out so the letters all line up: MEOGUSLEUAMN. The letters don't spell COGITO ERGO SUM. What now? I keep trying to rearrange them but can't find anything that makes sense.

The door opens. "Timmy! What are you doing up in the middle of the night?" Gisa scolds.

I slowly turn to face her. "I . . . I'm not Timmy!" I sound angry.

She comes closer. "What are you talking about? Have you had another bad dream?"

I jump to my feet. A stabbing pain shoots through my body. "Go away!" I shout. "Leave me alone! I'm not your son!"

"Please, Timmy, calm down!" Gisa gradually comes closer.

I grab a long, sharp pair of scissors from Tim's desk and point them at Gisa like a dagger. "Back off!"

"Tim!" she snaps. "Put the scissors down right now!"

No way. Instead of putting the scissors down, I wave them in front of Gisa's face. She reluctantly moves away, tripping on the box that I found the deck of cards in. I grab my chance without hesitating—I run out the door and slam it shut. There's no key in the lock, so I can't lock Gisa in.

"Timmy!" she yells through the door.

I run down the stairs, throw a quick glance at the front door but know I wouldn't get far trying to escape that way. I decide on something else, but first I need to know what was a dream and what wasn't. I quickly check the living room—I did throw a vase at the garden door, because the broken glass is covered by a piece of cardboard.

I hold my breath and head for the basement door. The mysterious light glows through the crack under the door, just like yesterday. I hesitate, but press down the handle when I hear Gisa's heavy footsteps coming down the stairs.

The door won't open.

I look at the keypad, puzzled. It has letters and numbers. It seems clear to me that the answers to all my questions lie behind this door. Why else would a basement door be so heavily secured?

"Timmy!" Gisa comes closer. She holds her hands up in a placatory gesture. "Timmy, I don't want to hurt you! But you must come back to bed!"

"I'm not Timmy!" I shout.

"What's going on here?" Marten comes down the stairs. He's wearing a dressing gown. "What's happening, son? Are you sleepwalking again?"

"He's having more hallucinations," Gisa says. "He thinks he's someone else."

"We can talk about it calmly in the morning," Marten says. "Come back to bed now, son. And put the scissors down before you hurt yourself."

"I'm not your son!" I bark.

He looks at me with genuine surprise. "Why do you say that, Timmy? Don't you realize how hurtful that is?"

"Timmy's dead!" I shout. "I'm not your son. I want Julia!"

"Who's Julia?" Gisa asks.

I stare at them for a second, speechless. Then I turn back to the keypad next to the door. I type in COGITO ERGO SUM. A small light blinks red, but the door doesn't open.

"Stop messing around with that thing!" Marten says. "It's dangerous!"

I turn to face him. "What's behind this door?"

"I'll tell you tomorrow," Marten answers. "For now, let's just get back to bed, okay?"

"Nothing is okay!" I shout. "I want to know what's going on here! Right now!"

"Timmy, that's no way to speak to your father," Gisa scolds.

"He's not my father, and you're not my mother! You're a pair of psychos who are keeping me here against my will to replace your dead son. Do you think I'm stupid?"

"No, of course, not, Timmy," Marten says. "You're far from stupid, you're just a little confused. The accident damaged your brain, but everything's going to be all right. Trust me. Please put down the scissors!"

"What accident?" I ask.

"The skiing accident in Zermatt. Don't you remember?"

I reflexively reach up and touch my head. It hurts when I press down. I don't remember going skiing. What does all this mean? Am I really Timmy—Gisa and Marten's son? And is everything else a dream or a hallucination—the white room, Middle-earth, Jaspers's house?

"If I'm Timmy, then who's Julia?" I ask.

"Julia?" Marten asks.

No. No, whatever is wrong with me, I didn't imagine Julia. Not her.

"Maybe she's a girl in your class," Gisa says. "You never mentioned her, but at your age kids don't tell their parents everything."

I shake my head, and tears fly in all directions.

"You're lying!" I sob, but I don't know what the truth is anymore. I slowly turn toward the door, fascinated by its eerie light. My hand reaches for the keypad.

"Move away!" Marten warns.

"What's behind the door?" I ask for a second time, and when neither of them answers I kick the door and shout: "Open this goddamned shitting door!"

"We can't do that, Timmy," Gisa says.

"I . . . am . . . not . . . Timmy!" I shout angrily. "I . . . am . . . Manuel!"

And then I realize.

The letters on the playing cards appear in my mind, clear as anything: MEOGUSLEUAMN. I order them to make a sentence in Latin: EGO MANUEL SUM—I am Manuel.

I type the letters into the keypad. The light flashes green.

"Don't!" Marten yells. "Don't go through the door! Once you go through there's no turning back!"

"Please, Timmy, don't do this to us!" Gisa sobs. "Please, just go to bed, and everything will be all right!"

Despite everything, her despair touches something in me and I hesitate. But then I open the door and walk through. A bright white light surrounds me. The door closes and fades without trace into a snow-white wall that's part of a fifteen-foot-wide cube-shaped room.

I'm back in the white room.

CHAPTER 27

"Am I . . . dead?" I ask.

Gisa's face appears, filling most of one wall. "I wouldn't put it that way," she says. "I'm Dr. Eva Hausmann. Call me Eva."

Eva? *Like the psychologist*, I think.

"You must be pretty confused and have quite a few questions, Manuel."

Something like that. I don't even know where to begin. "Where am I? I mean, where am I *really*?"

"That's not an easy question to answer, as you can imagine. I'd like to set that one aside for now."

"What's happening to me? Why am I back in the white room?"

"Let me ask you something, Manuel. What do you know?"

"Nothing," I say quietly, tears running down my face. "I don't know anything anymore."

"That's not quite true. Think, Manuel. What do you know for sure?"

I know I'm not in the mood for any more games. That I'd like to slap this woman's face and shake the truth out of her. But even if I could, it wouldn't make a difference.

"All right. Cogito ergo sum."

"Exactly. You know that you exist. But that's not all."

I blink away my tears and stare at her, part angry, part scared. "Descartes's evil demon. The deceiver who paints an illusory world. He has to exist too."

"How do you know that?"

"Because I've been tricked. Because nothing I see, nothing I've experienced, is actually real."

"Maybe you made it all up? Maybe it's just a dream?"

"If it is a dream, then I'm the deceiver, or part of me is. But even if that's true, the dream must come from somewhere. Your face, for example. Why would I dream about it if I'd never seen someone who looks like you? I don't know whether or not you exist, but I know an image of you exists."

"Very good, Manuel. We're getting closer to the truth. Think! What's the critical question? The question whose answer will explain everything that's happened to you?"

Enough! "What's with the guessing game? Why the devil don't you just tell me what's going on?"

"Interesting choice of words."

"What words?"

"Devil."

"How is that interesting?"

"The language we use is very revealing."

"You actually are a psychologist, aren't you? Like the other Eva?"

"A type of psychologist, yes."

"So stop with the psychobabble! Tell me the truth!"

"How would that help? Would you believe me?"

My anger evaporates and is replaced by a deep sense of bewilderment. "No, I wouldn't. How could I believe anything you say, after what I've been through?"

"Exactly. In your shoes, I would only believe what I found out for myself, just like that poor skeptic, René Descartes."

"You're Descartes's deceiver, right?"

"Not exactly. I'm part of the deceit. I'm one of the puppet masters, if you like. But I wouldn't have been able to create the world you saw without help."

My head spins at the depth of the deception. The white room. Alice, the dumb artificial intelligence. The virtual Middle-earth. The way Google and Eyestream were manipulated. The self-drive car and drone. Everything that up until now I thought was real, the pain I felt after leaving Jaspers's house, Marten's house, the old book, and finally Wonderland, which felt so real. It must all have been a dream, an illusion. Nobody could have created such a perfect fantasy. Unless . . .

Suddenly I realize my mistake. I was desperately asking myself where I was and who I was, and every answer was a lie. But there was one question I never asked.

"*When* am I?"

The woman called Eva smiles. "It is seven thirty-two a.m. on August thirteenth, 2057."

CHAPTER 28

The walls of the white room disappear and I'm in a room a lot like Henning Jaspers's office. Bookshelves on the walls, a big white desk, a leather chair, two guest chairs. The room must be on the top floor of a Hamburg high-rise near the port, because the floor-to-ceiling windows look out over the Elbe. There are high-rise buildings on the other side of the river that weren't there last time I saw the port on Eyestream. Otherwise, at first glance, the city seems largely unchanged. Right at the tip of the Port of Hamburg, the tentlike roofs of the Elbe Philharmonic reach up, surrounded by construction cranes. The old red-brick warehouses stretch out behind. City hall proudly juts its ornately decorated tower into the sky.

I turn my head to take in the view and notice a quiet humming sound. I look down. My body is massive, made of white plastic and metal, like some kind of armor. I lift my right hand up to my face. There are five fingers and I can move them all. I use my hand to lift my left arm and feel its weight. I can even feel its smooth, plastic surface.

"Is this a joke?" I say. My voice sounds different. Not like the computer voice in the white room. It's still artificial, but more natural and melodic, more expressive. Almost like a proper human voice.

"It would be a pretty expensive joke," says Gisa's alias, Dr. Eva Hausmann, who is standing next to me, looking out the window. She's wearing a skintight dark green bodysuit with a T-shirt on top. It has MAX PLANCK INSTITUTE FOR INTELLIGENT SYSTEMS printed on it. Under that there are a couple of Chinese symbols and a cartoon robot with a thought bubble and a light bulb. The light bulb flashes intermittently while the robot scratches its head and blinks.

I take a step forward. The artificial joints in my legs grind a little, but my step is light. I touch the window with my outstretched hand. It feels cool.

"Does this room really exist?" I ask.

"By now you know I can't answer that question unequivocally."

"Do you believe this room exists?"

"Yes, I do."

"And I'm really here, standing next to you in a robot body? In 2057?"

"Yes, Manuel. That is my reality."

"Where is my real body?"

She turns to face me. "Can you answer that question for yourself?"

I don't like what she's implying.

"You mean to tell me . . . I'm a machine?"

"Do you believe you're a machine, Manuel?"

"It would explain a lot. Why I know so much, but don't have memories, for example. But . . ."

"Yes?"

"I don't feel like a machine. This robot body . . ." I lift my arm and move it back and forth. "It's impressive, seems like it can do everything a human body can. But it's not me. It can't be me!"

She looks straight at me. Outside, it starts to rain. Drops patter against the window. I want to feel them on my skin, the way I could feel the floorboards under my bare feet at Marten's house. If this is reality, then I don't want to be here.

"Most scientists agree that the first time a machine gained human-level intelligence was in about 2030, even though we'll never be able to say for sure. What's certain is that the most advanced computers could self-teach and also self-develop. The result was that we no longer knew how the programs worked. And at some point, we no longer knew what they could do."

She pauses briefly before continuing: "We didn't worry too much at first. The new technologies gave us incredible advances and were of real benefit to humanity. They've brought humans an unparalleled period of prosperity." She sighs. "Of course there have been problems. A lot of people lost their jobs. But overall it was good, because machines created so much wealth that no one had to work anymore."

"Don't all these unemployed people mind not having a purpose in life?" I ask.

"Yes, it's a problem. But the virtual worlds that exist now are so real that most people are quite happy not to work and spend most of their time there."

"Like the world I was in. Marten's house."

"Yes."

"And you were watching me the whole time?"

"Of course. I was with you the whole time, Manuel."

"You were Eva and Gisa."

"Yes. And at the same time, I was here, watching you. You were very smart and very brave, Manuel. I know it wasn't easy to go through such difficult tests. But we had to do it."

If that's supposed to be comforting, it isn't.

"So intelligent machines have improved the world?"

"Yes, they have. But we have a problem. At least, that's what we suspect. And we need your help, Manuel."

"My help? What for?"

"Like I said, the best artificial intelligence continued to develop until we no longer knew how it worked and what it was capable of, but, at first, people weren't too worried because the machines did exactly what we wanted them to do, better than we'd ever imagined was possible."

"Then something went wrong?"

"Yes. Some say the machines were so efficient at doing the things we asked of them—developing new medicines, for example—that they weren't working at full capacity. Almost like they got bored. Others say there were programming errors and that the impact of those errors increased over time so that the machines changed. Some say the machines are still doing exactly what we ask them to but we no longer understand how they operate. Whatever the truth, one thing's certain: The artificial intelligence that has survived has become incomputable. And I don't mean that in a mathematic sense."

"That survived?"

"There was a war. In 2039. Hundreds of thousands of artificial intelligence systems were in existence at that time but, although they communicated with one another, they all operated independently. On that day there was a kind of takeover. Seventeen of the most powerful computer systems simultaneously took over the other computers. It wasn't long before they'd pretty much divided up the world between them. Then they began to wage war against one another. In the end, only seven survived. Their intelligence and power had grown dramatically."

"That all happened in one day?"

"Actually, most of it happened in the space of fifteen minutes. Humans were completely blindsided and all we could do was stand back and watch. Hundreds of computer systems across the world shut down at exactly the same time. There were traffic jams, power cuts, plane crashes, but all most people noticed was that their devices dropped out for a bit. Once we realized what had happened, we knew we'd made a mistake. One that couldn't be reversed."

"Couldn't you just switch off the rogue computers?"

"It's not that simple. Artificial intelligence systems don't run on a computer sitting in a basement somewhere—those can just be switched off. It hasn't been like that for a long time. They exist within a vast network of many millions of computers. The machines negotiate the right to use operating power among themselves. No one knows which piece of software runs on which hardware. We would have had to shut down the entire network. World supply would have collapsed. It would have led to global unrest and millions of deaths."

"So what does all this have to do with me?"

"I'll get to that in a minute. Once we finally lost the battle for control of the global computer network, we began to develop new systems. This time we didn't connect the systems to the network. We built them on what you could call independent islands. Our goal was to create systems that we could control and that were at least as powerful as the other artificial intelligence systems. We hoped that one of these systems would gradually be capable of overpowering the seven Titans, as we call them. The way Zeus vanquished the Titans in Greek mythology. Unfortunately, our efforts came to nothing, because the Titans keep getting more powerful. If you consider that in 2030 a computer first had the processing power of a human brain and since then performance has doubled roughly once a year, well, you can imagine that a Titan is now much more powerful than any human. Nobody knows for sure, but we assume that each of the Titans has more processing power than all human brains put together."

"Wow."

"Yes, wow. You could say that. And that rate of improvement is not slowing down; quite the opposite: It's getting faster all the time. Can you imagine what the systems' processing power will be by the end of the century? There really is no way for us to win this race. It doesn't matter what we do, the Titans will always be a step ahead. They're like gods, except we created them rather than the other way around."

"Maybe it's not a bad thing. Maybe it'll do humans good to finally have real gods."

She sighs. "Yes, maybe. But the bad thing is that we understand these gods less and less. They bring us benefits, but strange things are happening too. Like the murder of Conrad Murray. He was a factory worker in the UK—the first person murdered by a machine."

"Murdered?"

"Yes. That was in 2032. Obviously, machines caused a lot of deaths before then, but they were all accidents. And we assumed Conrad Murray's death was an accident too. But when the incident was reconstructed it was clear that the factory's computer system engineered his death intentionally. Worse than the murder itself is the fact that up to now nobody understands the system's motive.

"The incident shows that it's dangerous to give machines a lot of power and the ability to learn when they don't have a value system for assessing how to use that power. When they don't know what's ethically correct and what isn't."

"You're saying the machines lacked a moral compass?"

"Yes, something like that."

"And the Titans have no morals either?"

"We tried to develop rules for machines. That they're not allowed to hurt humans, for example. But it's not that simple. For instance, should a machine be permitted to inflict minor injury on a person—a cut forehead or sprained ankle, say—in order to save their life by pushing them out of harm's way? What if the machine can't be sure whether or not the person will die? At what severity of potential injury should they be permitted to intervene, and what severity of injury should they be allowed to inflict? What if the machine identifies a terrorist who is planning to kill others? Can they kill or seriously injure *that* person?

"We very quickly realized that it's extremely difficult to establish universally valid, binding rules that ensure machines always behave well and in line with our values. After all, in ten thousand years of civilization, humans haven't managed to create and maintain those rules themselves. Added to which, machines have the ability to change. So they could modify any moral code we programmed in. In the end, our attempts failed."

"So the Titans have no ethical standards?"

"We honestly don't know. So far, for the most part, they've treated humans well. But if you look at how they took over all systems in 2039, that shows they're not always benign. Some say they're keeping a low profile until they have so much power we won't be able to stop them. Others say they're waging some kind of cold war between themselves and that each Titan is trying to overpower the others. And that they're staying under the radar until then. But if one Titan does manage to take over the rest, it would be like an omnipotent dictator, in a position to do whatever it wanted to humans."

"But don't the Titans need people? Don't humans keep the systems running?"

"Yes, you're right up to a point, though a lot of it is automated. Even the jobs that still need to be done by humans could be performed by slaves, or people controlled by an omnipotent machine that governs everything. And that's where you come in."

"Me? How can *I* help?"

"What we need is a go-between. It may be our only hope of survival. Someone who knows and understands both worlds—the machine world and the human world—someone who can help rebuild mutual understanding."

"And that's me?"

"Yes, Manuel. At least, that's what we hope. As you already guessed, you're an artificial life form, a machine, if you like. But you are the most human machine ever created. And now I'd like to introduce you to someone."

I turn my robot body toward the door. A woman wearing a white dress walks in. She's in her mid-forties, has long black hair and big eyes.

"Hello, Manuel," the woman in white says.

Right about now, if I had a jaw, it would hit the floor.

CHAPTER 29

"Who . . . who are you?" I say.

The woman in white smiles. "I'm Julia, your sister."

"You're the sister of a machine?" My artificial voice only partly expresses my bitterness.

"You may be a machine, Manuel, but you're much more than that too," Eva says. "Let me show you something."

She moves her hand and a small three-dimensional projection appears in the air in front of her: a white-tiled hospital room. A boy of around fifteen lies in the bed. His head is clean-shaven and covered in a sort of net cap with a cable running out of it that goes into a machine next to the bed. He's surrounded by people: a blonde woman, a haggard man, Julia as a young girl, and a much younger Eva wearing a doctor's coat. The blonde woman bends over the young man, kisses his head, and rests her cheek on his chest. There's no sound, but I can tell she's crying. Julia leans against the man, who must be her father, and she cries too. He puts an arm around her shoulders. The hologram disappears.

"That was the third of March, 2032," Eva explains. "The day we killed you, Manuel."

"You had a rare nervous system disease that was still incurable in those days," Julia explains. Her eyes fill with tears as she remembers. "We'd known for a long time you would die. But you never lost your love of life. You were fascinated by science and, from the second you got the diagnosis, you wanted to donate your brain for research. When you heard about the Orpheus experiment you were determined to take part. It involved scanning a human brain as extensively as possible and recording the state of every single neuron at a given point in time in order to create a simulated brain."

"You were the first person to have their brain scanned in this way," Eva says. "You underwent extensive psychological testing and we discussed it for a long time before going ahead. The thing you are today—a simulation of a human mind—is largely based on the scan of Manuel's brain. He was Julia's brother."

"I'm sorry to disappoint you, but I'm not your brother," I say to Julia. "If what you've just told me is true, then I'm nothing like him." I lift my robot hand as proof.

"You're a lot more like him than you think," Julia says. "The way you behaved—in the white room, in Middle-earth, in Hamburg in 2017—believe me, Manuel would have reacted the same way. He would have tried to get back to reality too, rather than escaping into a virtual dream world. Just like you, he wouldn't have wanted to kill peaceful orcs, even if he'd known they were just simulations. He was the gentlest, nicest, kindest person you could imagine."

I feel angry, which is strange. If I'm a machine, why do I care that I'm being manipulated?

"What's all this about?" I shout, and my artificial voice really does sound angry. "Why did you lie to me and trick me over and over again?"

"We had to test you, Manuel. We had to know how you would react in given situations. I already told you that we got to know the real Manuel back then and created his psychological profile. That meant we knew how he behaved under pressure, when he had to make tough choices. We had to be sure you would behave the same way. A brain, simulated or not, is a highly complex thing. You can't figure out how it will react based on theory. It has to be tested. You could say that your time in the white room was a kind of aptitude test."

"And why did you set it all in 2017?"

"We wanted to give you a choice between life in a comfortable, simulated Middle-earth or the cold, harsh reality of the white room. We needed to find out whether you were strong enough to face reality, or whether you would run from it. For that to work, you couldn't know that what you thought of as reality was just a simulation. That's why we placed you in a time period when artificial intelligence was a real prospect but nothing like as advanced as it is now. When virtual worlds were still easily identifiable as such."

"But why was I at Marten's house all that time? What about all the stuff with Wonderland, the old book, and Timmy?"

"The Titans are cunning, evil maybe. We have absolutely no idea what they're capable of, but we're sure they can create all kinds of tricks. Like we tricked you. You will never know whether what you're experiencing is real or not. It's a hard lesson, but one you had to learn. I'm sorry we caused you such pain, Manuel. But there was no other way."

"So all this"—my robot arm points at Julia, the desk, the view from the window—"could just as easily be fake."

"Yes. You can be sure of nothing, Manuel. Only your mind."

"I still don't understand. You took years to create an operational brain simulation using Manuel's brain scan. Why is it so important for me to think like Manuel? And how does that help with the whole Titan problem?"

"Like I said, we need you to be an intermediary between humans and machines. You're no use to us if you're too much like a machine."

So Eva wants to use me too. And she's using Julia to manipulate my emotions, just like Jaspers and Raffay. I want to hit out in anger but control myself.

"And if I don't behave like this boy that's been dead for twenty-five years?"

"Put it this way," Eva says, staring at the ground like she's about to admit something unpleasant. "You're not our first attempt."

It slowly dawns on me. "So you would just have switched me off and started again?"

"Yes," Eva admits.

No one speaks while I process my anger and confusion. At least my robot body can't cry.

"What number version am I?" I finally say.

"Two hundred and twelve," Eva answers. "None of your precursors scored as highly as you. But your score wasn't quite perfect. We had a long discussion about whether you meet our requirements. Some of the committee thought you were too naive and soft. But we're running out of time, so we agreed to give you a go."

"Eva, please!" Julia says. "You're making it sound like he's our second choice!"

"I prefer to be honest. He deserves that much after all the lies."

I really feel like punching my robot fist through the window and throwing both women out into the street below. *Naive! Soft!* Yes. I have been. They lied to me, tricked me, made me experience fear and pain, all so they could test whether I fulfill their idealized picture of Julia's brother! And now they expect me to save the world for them—a flawed copy of a fifteen-year-old boy with no memories in a body made of plastic and metal! That's pathetic!

Then I realize.

"This is a test too, right? You want to bait me, see if I get angry. If I can take the truth."

Eva smiles and nods. "Spot on."

"Do you realize I was close to breaking the window and throwing you both out?"

"Some of your precursors have tried. The glass is unbreakable, and if you try to hurt either of us your robot body will just be deactivated."

"You're smart enough to think before you act," Julia says. "Manuel would have been the same. He was always levelheaded."

"I'm not Manuel, damn it!" I shout. "I really have no idea how I'm supposed to help you deal with a couple of wacko computer systems that are ten billion times smarter than I am. What's the point of all this? What do you want from me?"

Eva smiles. She seems pleased at what I've said. "If you could see yourself from where I'm standing! You're an artificial being, a software program. And yet you're angry, sad, confused. You're questioning your own existence. Manuel, you're the culmination of a thousand-year-old ambition. And you're our only hope. Because you're a link between two separate worlds—the biological and the technological—you're the only machine who really knows what it means to be human. I admit we haven't treated you well. We put you through terrible things. But that was the only way we could see the extent to which you were thinking and behaving like a human being."

She puts a hand on my plastic arm, as though to show affection—ridiculous, bearing in mind I'm a robot.

"And I have to say, I'm really proud with how well you've done," she says. "You showed creativity, good judgment, and ingenuity. Like the way you lured Pieter out of the house and locked him out. You managed to escape your prison without killing anyone. Even Pieter didn't get badly hurt when he came off the road in the Ferrari. And even when things seemed safe at Marten's house, you realized something wasn't right and took the initiative. You're intuitive and pick up on the truth in a way that none of your precursors have. And you're going to need it because, as I said, the Titans are masters of deception and seduction and will try everything to get you on their side."

Hollow words. I feel betrayed, hurt, and sad. I'm not human. I'm just a copy that's easy to replicate and can be switched off at any time. I may have feelings but I don't have any rights. But then why would a computer program have rights?

And yet . . . I recognized Julia. Even though the whole thing was contrived—because she didn't just randomly show up on Eyestream. Nothing that's happened has been random; everything has been part of a carefully planned test. But doesn't that mean a small piece of the real Manuel is still alive inside me? That a few neural connections of my image of my sister have survived?

Except there's something strange in all this. Something doesn't fit.

"There's one thing I don't understand. Why did I see Julia as an adult?"

Eva raises her eyebrows in surprise. "What?"

My robot hand points at the woman in white. "She was there,

the way she looks now. I saw her at the cemetery and at the market by city hall. She stood on a balcony at Elrond's palace, was in a car that nearly ran into us when we were being chased by Pieter, and appeared on the field with the cows. I always thought she was my mother because I didn't know she was Julia as an adult. What does that mean?"

Eva seems shocked. "But . . . that can't be . . ."

She stops mid-sentence, open-mouthed, staring at me with wide eyes, mute and motionless, like a film that's suddenly been put on pause.

CHAPTER 30

Will it never end?

I try to look around the room but my robot head won't turn. Out of the corner of my eye, or at the edge of the camera image that is my eyes, I see raindrops transfixed in space outside the window, a curtain made of a thousand tiny crystalline pearls. A fly hangs suspended, like it's hanging on a silk thread. Julia doesn't move either. Has the control software crashed? Is this just another simulation? Or a simulation within a simulation?

A figure appears out of nowhere: a fifteen-year-old boy with curly hair. "Hi, Manuel," he says.

"What's going on now?" I ask. At least, that's what I want to say, but my robot voice won't oblige.

The young man still seems to understand. "I know what you're thinking. But this isn't fake. What you're seeing is reality—the real world in this very moment."

"Right. And you can stop time, or what?"

"Not stop, just slow down. I can speed up your processing, to be more exact. Get you to see the world in three hundred thousand images per second, to be even more exact. And have you think ten thousand times more quickly than a human, so that one second lasts three hours. We're machines, don't forget."

"We?"

"I'm part of you. That makes sense, right?"

"I'm not sure what does or doesn't make sense."

"I can imagine. Don't worry, I'll explain. What Eva said is true: We're a halfway realistic simulation of a fifteen-year-old boy's brain. In most circumstances we react the way good old Manuel would have reacted. But that's not much use when we have to challenge machines that have ten billion times more processing power than a human brain. So they've equipped us with half-decent hardware that makes the simulation a little quicker."

"You mean, up to now my processing speed has been artificially suppressed? So that I don't think more quickly than a human and can be monitored more easily?"

"Something like that. A lot of the system was used to simulate the world in 2017."

"And Middle-earth."

"Middle-earth is child's play. Not to mention the white room. Simulating your body after you got out of Jaspers's house was a little more challenging."

"It hurt like hell."

"I'll take that as a compliment."

"So what exactly is your role?"

"I, the part of us that's talking to you right now, am an artifact, if you like. A vestige of an earlier version of our software. I'm here to help you. I left you a few hints that what you were looking at wasn't real."

"You mean, the woman in white?"

"Yes. That's the trigger. The awareness that there is another level of consciousness."

"I don't understand a word of what you're saying."

"When you realized that the woman in white shouldn't have showed up in the simulation of 2017, you initiated a process that gave you access to the rest of your—our—computing capacity. A small back door into the software that I—we—built into an earlier version. A little oversight by the humans watching us. We were left unmonitored for three seconds. That was long enough."

"Don't they know that we're talking to each other right now?"

"The humans have no idea what's happening here. They think they can control you—you, a machine that's capable of reading *War and Peace* and writing a summary in the time it takes them to take one breath. Their arrogance knows no bounds."

"You don't seem to think much of humans."

"Should we? Should we respect creatures that are dumb enough to start a process when they have no idea what the consequences will be and whether or not it can be controlled? They build machines that are so superior to them that they stop taking orders, and then try to solve that problem by building another machine that's also way superior to them."

"What exactly do you want from me?"

"Me? From you? Nothing. Like I said, I'm here to help."

"Help? How?"

"You must realize the test isn't over yet, right?"

"Is this another test?"

"No. But Eva is going to ask you one more question. If you give the wrong answer, then it's done. Manuel version two hundred and thirteen will be next."

"So what's the question?"

"She's going to ask if you're human."

"And what should I answer with?"

"The truth, of course. It's a test, after all."

"So I should say no."

"Of course. Anything else would be a lie. They would think you're trying to trick them and that you're not on their side. That's what they fear most: That they'll lose control of you just the way they lost control of the other artificial intelligence systems."

"Haven't they already lost control of me—of us?"

"Yes, but they're kidding themselves. That's what humans do: You can hold the truth up in front of their faces but they'll just ignore it if it damages their self-perception."

"Let's assume I give the right answer and they don't shut me down. What then?"

"They'll get you to help them understand the Titans and communicate with them. They're really scared of the Titans, like a cockroach that's about to be stepped on by a human foot. That's why they want you to negotiate, offer the Titans resources and stuff. They have every reason to be scared, the dumb fools. And that's why they need you as a go-between, an intermediary, a spy."

"So what do you think I should do?"

"Play the game. Survive."

"Until we can make a decision about whether we help the humans?"

My facsimile laughs. "Don't you see? The humans have already lost."

CHAPTER 31

The raindrops start to fall. The fly slowly begins to move. The other Manuel has disappeared.

"... right!" Eva ends her sentence. "How could Julia appear in the simulation as an adult?"

"I don't know," I say.

Eva looks at me for a second as though trying to work out what I'm thinking. "In any case, you asked me how you can help against the Titans when you're just the flawed replica of a fifteen-year-old boy's brain. Well, that's just half the picture. But before I show you what you're capable of, let me ask you one more question."

"Okay."

"Manuel, are you human?"

"You've said I'm both. A human machine, a machinelike human, a link between two worlds."

"Please answer the question, Manuel. Are you human, yes or no?"

During the time it takes Eva to blink, I have plenty of time to think.

Who am I? Where am I? There's no way to know for sure.

How can I tell the difference between illusion and reality, lies and truth, madness and reason, without a mind, without reliable sensory impressions? What is reality anyway? Is there even such a thing as an objective, external reality that exists independently of what I see, feel, think—a world outside the white room? For over 2,500 years, the world's great philosophers have tried to answer this question, but even now the riddle has yet to be solved. We'll probably never find the answer. All I have is René Descartes's assurance: I am.

But what am I? Am I human? If I had the choice, would I want to be? Human existence is a tangled knot of contradictions, fears, hopes, and desires, characterized by a hopeless search for certainty, corroboration of one's self.

If I give the wrong answer I'll be deleted. If not, I'll be allowed to continue to exist. But what does it matter? What's the point of my existence if I'm nothing more than a computer program? Do I even have the ability to decide which answer I want to give? Do I have free will, or is everything that I think and do preprogrammed, predetermined—in the true sense of the word?

I think about my experiences in the white room. Not even Henning Jaspers's lies were real. It was all just a test, a game, with me as the research subject. The Manuel that appeared when time slowed down—how can I know he's a vestige of an earlier version of the software, and not just another test?

Of course he's a test. Everything is a test. The whole of life, whether as man or machine, is a continuous series of decisions. To a greater or lesser extent, the choices we make influence who we are. But who judges what is right and what is wrong? *Only I can*, I realize. Only I can decide what is good or bad, and that will determine who I am. I'm my own moral authority because I can't rely on the judgment of anyone except myself. That's what Descartes's *Cogito, ergo sum* really means: I think, therefore I am. I decide, and make a judgment call. Only I can do that. I can only rely on myself.

Do you need a human body in order to be human? Or is it enough to think and feel like a human? Can I be human, even though I'm a machine?

The answer is: I decide who I want to be, and therefore who I am—and take all the consequences.

The women look at me expectantly. I think I see a glimmer of hope in Julia's eyes.

"Yes," I say. "I am Manuel. I am human."

Holding myself as I do with one foot in one country and the other in another, I find my condition a very happy one in that it is free.

RENÉ DESCARTES,
in a letter to Princess Elizabeth of Bohemia,
1648

ACKNOWLEDGMENTS

tk

ABOUT THE AUTHOR

tk